SANDY ROSE

THERESA SEIFERT

Page Solutions - Prowriters Network
541 Buttermilk Pike
Crescent Springs, KY 41017

ISBN 979-8-89633-025-7 (softcover)
ISBN 979-8-89633-026-4 (ebook)

This book is a work of fiction. Names, characters, places, and incidents are the product of the author's imagination or are used fictitiously. Any resemblance to actual locales, events, or persons, living or dead, is purely coincidental.

Printed in the United States of America.

My name is Theresa Seifert. I am seventy-one years old, and this is my first book. I grew up with a learning disability. They told my mother I was unable to learn in a normal fashion. They wanted to put me into special classes for children that had difficulty learning. My mother stood firm and refused to let them transfer me. Thank God for my mother! I struggled all through school. It took me fourteen years to finally graduate. I became a cosmetologist and had a successful career for thirty-four years. I was married to my husband, John Seifert, for twenty-five years. He developed leukemia and died after a bone marrow transplant at the age of forty-seven. I've been a widow for twenty-three years. Now that I'm retired, I hope to fulfill a lifelong dream: writing a book and having it published.

In the beginning, Sandy and I were born as conjoint twins. We were joined at the back of the head. I was small and frail with not much of a chance to survive. She was much bigger and healthy, so the decision was made that I would be sacrificed to save her. Part of me lived on. I was tucked away in the back of her brain, always seeing and knowing her every thought. I tried to be the voice of reason, but that rarely ever worked. All I could do was to watch. Now I'll tell her story. I am the only one who really knows what happened.

1

The rain came down in sheets. The wind blew cold against her skin. The underbrush scraped her bare flesh as she ran deeper into the woods. She fell to the ground, the empty pill bottle still clutched in her hand and the whiskey bottle lay empty by her side. Blood dripped from the cuts into her half-opened eyes. She whispered softly to herself as she closed them, "I won't wake up. The nightmare will be over." It was her twenty-eighth birthday.

Her life had been a roller coaster from childhood. Her mother was an alcoholic schizophrenic. Her father had tried everything to help her. She had been in and out of rehabs. She saw several different psychiatrists and had even tried group therapy. Even with all that effort, nothing seemed to help. Sandy came home from school one day to find her mother covered in blood. She had taken tweezers and plucked the flesh from between her eyes until she hit the bone. I know the real reason. She never forgave herself for sacrificing me. She called me a Rose. They never really officially named me. Mother came back a few weeks after my burial and planted a yellow rose of Texas at my grave. In her mind, when she thought of me, she called me Rose.

Father became a workaholic, trying to keep up with the mounting bills. He finally worked himself into an early grave. He died the year Sandy graduated. Mother had a complete breakdown and had to be institutionalized.

The boy-next-door John and Sandy had been dating for two years. He had been her first sexual experience. The very first time she had a climax, she was amazed at how wonderful it felt. They had had sex almost every day. When he asked her to marry him, she felt it was her only choice. There wasn't any inheritance. The house was being auctioned by the bank. She had sixty days to get out. Marrying him, she wouldn't be homeless. She wasn't sure she loved him. She wasn't even sure that she knew what love was. There didn't seem to be any between her parents. She never saw them kiss or have any compassion toward one another, only fighting, confusion, and despair.

Sandy and John got married at the justice of the peace. Only a few friends attended. Things were rocky from the very start. He turned out to be not only a jerk but unfaithful. He had given her the crabs. She had never been so embarrassed to go to her family doctor. He prescribed a salve that you would rub on the affected area. She got back at him by telling him the only way to get rid of crabs was to shave his entire torso. She put itching powder into the salve that he rubbed on his balls. Watching him go crazy running around the bathroom scratching like the dog he was, she laughed so hard she wet her pants. Things didn't last much longer. They were divorced within two years.

2

She was beautiful, buxom with blond hair and blue eyes. You would think these traits would have been a blessing, but occasionally, she felt as if they were a curse. All kinds of men were attracted to her. She had developed a strong sex drive and a taste for alcohol. That combination made for many bad decisions. Most of the men she went out with turned out to be jerks like her husband. She drifted through relationship after relationship, some very short and some a little longer. The days turned into months, and the months turned into years. Still her knight in shining armor was nowhere to be found. Her prince didn't have to ride on a white stallion. His armor would be a business suit; his treasures, a bank account and a decent home. She daydreamed of him having a big dick. They didn't have to live in a palace, just something better than the room she was renting from a friend.

One afternoon, a girlfriend named Terry invited her to lunch to meet her dentist, Lukas. From the moment they sat down, she started playing footsie under the table, rubbing his leg with her bare foot as close to his crotch as she could reach. She was sweating all over; her neck turned red. That's what happened when she started to feel that insatiable appetite take over. She could feel that he was getting hard. That just excited her more. After lunch, he canceled all his afternoon appointments. They bid Terry goodbye and raced toward the van. Reaching it, they wasted no time removing their clothes. She hopped on top. Sweat poured down her body, dripping onto him. The van rocked back and forth. Suddenly, the air was filled with moans and screams of joy and ecstasy. Having leather seats certainly was a blessing.

They were inseparable from that point on. They had sex in his office, in restaurants, in bathrooms, and in bars.

The first few weeks were like being on an endless honeymoon. She had a habit of giving men in her life a nickname. She finally called him Mr. Extra Big. They spent their days working, but at night, it was an endless marathon of raw sex. Nothing was off limits. They had truly met their soul mate. They were Mr. and Mrs. Jekyll in the day and Mr. and Mrs. Hyde at night.

She came home one day with a backache from standing on her feet, leaning over a shampoo booth for ten hours. He greeted her at the door with a passionate kiss.

"What's up, baby?"

She gave him a half smile. "I'm in pain. My back is killing me."

"I have something that will fix you right up." He poured her a drink as she sat down. He leaned over and gave her another kiss. "I'll be right back." When he returned, he handed her a painkiller. It was the first time she had taken one. She had no idea that this combination could be deadly.

She soon learned a couple of drinks and a painkiller gave her that feeling of euphoria. Only sex had done that in the past. She thought that being a doctor he had an endless supply but soon realized that wasn't the case. He kept a bottle of them at home, which she had been dipping into quite frequently. One evening, he had a splitting headache. He went to take one. The bottle only has a few left.

He confronted her, "Have you been taking them without asking me?" He shook his head and in a very cool manner said, "That's not right." She told him her back had been hurting. She didn't think she needed his permission. "No wonder you've been in such a good mood and I thought it was me."

It was late one night. Mr. X had a few extra drinks and fell asleep on the couch. She was desperate, not only wanting but needing that feeling. She slipped out of the house and drove to his office. She had taken his keys. Letting herself in, she didn't turn the lights on. She knew his office like the back of her hand. Going to the dispensary, she found a locked cabinet She took one of the dental tools and broke it open. There they were in all their glory, two large bottles holding a hundred apiece. Slipping them into her jacket pocket, she found some tissues. Wiping her fingerprints from everything that she had touched, she put the tool back and made her way to the door. She realized this wouldn't work. It had to look like a break-in. Going to the trunk of her car, she got part of the jack handle and used it to jimmy the door.

Driving home, she was shaking. She'd never been so nervous. She took one of the pills and let it dissolve in her mouth with nothing to drink. It left a bitter taste. Pulling into the driveway, she said a little prayer, hoping Mr. X would still be sleeping. Opening the door, she could hear him lightly snoring. She tiptoed through the house, turning the clocks back an hour. She turned the TV off and then woke him gently.

"You have been sleeping for a half an hour. Don't you want to go to bed?"

He glanced at the clock. It was only ten thirty. He was rested and horny as a son of a bitch. She was so relieved that she had not been caught. She would give him the ride of a lifetime. He fell asleep almost immediately after coming. She got out of bed and turned the clocks to the correct time. It had been quite a night. She was mentally and physically exhausted. She curled up beside him and fell into a deep sleep.

Mr. X called her at work the next day. "There has been a break-in at my office. Someone stole the drugs. You don't know anything about that, do you?"

"Of course not. I was with you all night. You know that."

That was right. He had only fallen asleep for a half an hour. That would not have been enough time. "The police have been asking questions. You do understand I had to ask you."

She didn't appreciate being accused of something he knew she could not have done. He apologized, "I'm sorry, baby. I'll see you tonight. I love you."

"I love you too."

The receptionist at the office had a new boyfriend. He had been in trouble for drugs before. They assumed it was him, but with no fingerprints, no witnesses, no concrete evidence, no one was ever charged.

It would soon be her twenty-fifth birthday, and Mr. X had planned a party for her. Terry was a good friend of hers. They had worked together at the beauty shop for a couple of years. She didn't want to go. She was just recovering from the flu and felt like hell, but Sandy insisted it wouldn't be a party without her. They had an open bar, and if you were part of the inner circle, you could use the bathroom upstairs, which doubled for a safe place to share drugs. Cocaine was at the top of the list, but there was an assortment of uppers and downers—Valium, black beauties, white crosses, even heroin for a chosen few.

The girls from the shop had pitched in and bought her a cake in the shape of a dick with balls. Even the veins showed. It was a little unorthodox to bring it out at the beginning of the party. Some of the girls didn't mind having a drink, but being around a drug-induced atmosphere made them nervous. They surprised her with the cake. It had twenty-five candles on it, the kind that won't go out when you blow on them. They all had a good time watching her blow the cake—that is, everyone but Mr. X.

Terry didn't mind the atmosphere. She just wished she had felt better so she could have joined in.

She was sitting on the floor next to her. Sandy was eating a steak. It looked amazing. Terry hadn't been able to eat very much for a week. Sipping on a Coke, she was talking to her when she realized she wasn't answering. She looked at her eyes. They were glazed over.

She screamed, "Can you hear me?" No response. She had seen a person choking before so she jumped to her feet and immediately began screaming, "She's choking, she's choking!" A friend of theirs that worked at a restaurant jumped to his feet. He didn't know if she was drunk and passing out or she was really choking. The one thing that he did know if he didn't do something, Terry would have a heart attack. They got her on her feet. He began doing the Heimlich. He pulled her close and put his arms around her, thrusting hard and down on her diaphragm.

Terry looked at her. "Can you say anything?" No response. She yelled, "Do it again!"

Mr. X came up drunk, slurring his words. "Leave her alone. She's okay."

She told him to shut the fuck up. Looking at Bill, she screamed, "Don't stop!"

On the third push, the meat came flying out of her mouth. She slumped to the floor, gasping. "It was like being in a tunnel. I could hear you, but I couldn't move. I could feel my legs and arms going numb." She began to cry. You would have thought having this near-death experience would have made her think twice about getting so high, but it didn't.

At work the next day, a new girl was at the station next to Sandy's. She introduced herself, "I'm Sandy. I guess you're the newest member of the team."

"I'm Hope." She was a beauty with heart-shaped face and dark short hair that framed her large brown eyes. She had beautiful lips, white teeth, and a smile that would stop traffic.

"Hope, that's a nice name. It really suits you. Do you have a clientele, or are you fresh out of school?"

"I've been doing hair for years, and I have a pretty loyal client base that will follow me."

"Maybe you will bring some new life to the shop."

They would become instant friends. The shop was busy with all the new people. Passing in the hallway, Sandy asked if she could go to the bar next door and have a drink after work. Nodding her head yes, Hope looked quite comical like a bobble head.

Sandy asked, "Anybody waiting at home for you?"

Hope replied, "A jealous boyfriend, but he doesn't get home until eight. I'm kind of in the same boat, but he never knows how late I'll work. I can spin a tale even my mother would believe."

They left the shop at six and went to the bar. Everyone knew Sandy; she was a regular. She often went there after work for a drink before heading home.

"Do you drink martinis?"

"Yes! My favorite. I like them really dirty with two olives."

They ordered a round of drinks and toasted to their new friendship. They ordered another round; they laughed and joked and badmouthed their boyfriends. They ordered the third round. Sandy pulled money from her wallet to pay the bill. Hope got up.

"I have to go to the john. You want to come with me."

"Why? Do you need help."

Hope just giggled. "You know, it's a girl thing."

Entering the bathroom, Hope motioned to her to come in the stall. Encouraging her, she pulled out a little baggy that had white powder in it "You know what this is? Does a bear shit in the woods?"

Hope sprinkled some on the back of the toilet. She took out a credit card and started chopping. She handed Sandy a dollar.

"Roll it up like a straw." She cut two big lines. "This stuff is really good. We could drink three more martinis and never feel it." Hope took her finger and rubbed the residue on her gums. "I love the way it makes them feel numb just like the rest of me. One more round as they sipped them, Sandy gave Hope's knee a little squeeze.

"It's late. You only have twenty minutes to get home before the big bad wolf comes knocking."

Hope pulled up her shirt; there was a big black-and-blue mark. "What happened?"

"Yours likes kinky stuff. Mine likes to hit." Outside the bar, they hugged, simultaneously saying, "You're my new best buddy."

Sandy gave her a pinch. "Touch blue, you owe me a coke and I don't mean a soda."

On the way home, she felt all jittery inside; cocaine did that to her. She was afraid Mr. X would notice. She had a Valium in her purse, so she pulled the car over and found it in the comer of her bag. A half-empty bottle of water was in the holder. She took a sip and swished it around in her mouth as she swallowed. Mr. X was waiting for her. He had made his specialty for dinner: spaghetti. As they sat at the table, Sandy told him about her busy day.

"The owner hired a new girl. She brought a big clientele with her. It made everything run behind. Not enough dryers."

He poured her a glass of wine. She moved the food around like she was eating, taking a little bite every once in a while. He didn't seem to notice. He poured her another glass. Setting it down, he kissed her neck.

"I'm in the mood for some rough-and-tumble. Take a bath." She took her wine with her. She really wasn't in the mood for the bad-boy routine, but she did as she was told. When she entered the bedroom, there were handcuffs and a whip lying on the bed. She was glad that he was the one that wanted to be abused.

The next day at work, she kept looking at the clock; the day was dragging. It was the same old mundane routine. It was busy; there was no time for bathroom breaks, not even lunch. Talking over her customer, she got Hope's attention. She put her hand to her mouth and made a gesture as if she were drinking. Then she pointed to her nose. Hope gave her the thumbs-up.

When the day was finally over, they ran to the bar. Sandy said, "I love my job. I just wished their hair didn't come with a mouth and body. Having to listen to all the crap that goes on in their lives. It's very rare that I hear a good story." If they knew half of what was going on in her life, she probably would never see them again.

Sandy saw a familiar face across the bar. She wandered over. "Fancy meeting you here." It was her eye doctor smiling back.

"Well, fancy meeting you here. Are you alone?"

"No, I'm with one of the girls from the shop." They looked across the bar. "You don't mean that cute little brunette."

"Yeah, I do."

"Invite her over."

She motioned for Hope to join them. The bar was noisy. They found a table in the back. It was quieter there. They made small talk and he ordered round after round. Time passed quickly. Hope stood up and tripped over the leg of the chair.

"I think I've had more than I should have. Time to go home." Sandy put her arm around the eye doctor's shoulder.

"I think I'll stay a while longer. Mr. X won't be home until midnight."

"Are you sure?"

The doctor gave Hope a little wink. "I'll make sure she gets home safe and sound."

As Hope left, he ordered another round. By that time, Sandy knew she had really had her limit. He suggested that she follow him to his office. It was just a couple of blocks down the street. With the promise of some cocaine to help balance her out, she thought it would be safe to drive home. Funny how drugs and alcohol really do affect your judgment.

Entering the office, they made their way back to the last room. He took out a little brown bottle and shook white powder from it. He handed Sandy a little gold straw. "Help yourself."

She leaned down and snorted some of the powder from the pile. Taking the straw from her, he said, "It's my turn." He moved the straw back and forth, snorting up every last little bit. Immediately, she could feel her blood pulsing through her veins. Her heart was pounding in her chest and a warm tingling sensation filled her body head to toe.

"That's really good."

He took her hand and pulled her close. "I have a lot more of that if you could do me a favor."

"What would that be?"

He took a soda can from the counter and placed it under his hydraulic chair. "All you have to do is stand on my dick."

"What?"

He took his clothes off and lay back in his examining chair. He was hard. "Just stand on it. That's all you have to do." She took off her shoes and climbed on his lap, placing her feet on his hard dick. Standing up, she could barely keep her balance. Then he let the chair come down on the can. As the can was being smashed, he came all over her feet. She was shocked. She had never done anything like that before. He brought out the little brown bottle and poured another pile.

"That was fantastic. Anytime you want to do that again, just give me a call." She snorted the white powder then put her shoes on and left. She barely made it home before Mr. X arrived. She was high and drunk and horny. That was one of the most erotic and crazy experiences that she ever had. She attacked Mr. X as he came through the door. She led him to the bedroom and pushed him down on the bed.

"What's gotten into you?"

She simply said, "Quiet, no talking." She unzipped and pulled his pants off then his boxers. "Roll over on your side." By this time, he was hard with anticipation of what was to come. She took him into her mouth, swirling her tongue around the head of his penis, then firmly moving her hand up and down in a rhythmical manner. This made her feel like a real woman pleasing her man. The sweetness of his nectar filled her mouth and she swallowed. She had a climax. He didn't need to touch her. The sheer joy of pleasing him made her come. They lay on the bed, embracing, and fell asleep.

When the alarm went off, she wanted to roll back over and go to sleep. Dragging herself out of bed, she stumbled to the shower. The tepid water flowing over her body woke her to reality. Another day of work. Mr. X was gone. He had an early appointment. She went through the cabinets looking for any kind of a pill that she thought would help her through the day. Giving everything a nickname, she just called them her little helpers. She looked in his secret stash places that he didn't know she knew about. Her search was futile. Maybe Hope would have something.

She kept looking at the door waiting for Hope to arrive, but after a while, it was clear that she wasn't.

"What happened to Hope?"

One of her other coworkers said she was in a car accident. The day dragged. Her customers noticed that she wasn't her bubbly self. "Something wrong?"

She replied, "No, just not having the best of days." She swept up after her last haircut and went to the bar next door.

She thought about going by Hope's but decided that might not be a good idea. She ordered her regular. While she was waiting for it, she put her head in her hands. It was pounding. Her martini had arrived; she quickly gulped it down. She paid her bar tab and hurried to the parking rot. She thought of Dr. Can Crusher; she glanced at her watch. Maybe, just maybe, he would still be there. She put her car on cruise control so she wouldn't speed. Pulling into the lot, yes! His car was still there, but the office door was locked. She knocked. No response. She knocked harder. He came to the door with a puzzled look on his face; his clothes were disheveled.

"What are you doing here?"

"I thought you might be in the mood for a little fun."

"I was having fun until you bang the door down."

"Oh, you're not alone?"

"No!"

Her face turned pale. Her palms were sweating. She needed something and she needed it now. "Maybe you'd be up for a little three-way."

A smile came to his face. "I didn't know you were into things like that." Opening the door a little wider, she stepped inside. "Anybody I know?"

"I don't think so." She followed him back to the last room. On his examining chair sat a beautiful redhead with emerald green eyes and long hair. "I don't think you need a formal introduction."

Sandy excused herself to the restroom, "I need to freshen up a bit."

As she came out of the bathroom naked, her breasts bounced a little as she walked. She had shaved her whole body. The redhead had a full bush and small breasts. She was tall with flawless skin. She could have been a model.

He quickly took his clothes off. "Well, ladies, do you have any suggestions?"

Sandy saw the empty can on the counter. She placed it under his hydraulic chair. "Who wants to be on top?" The small-breasted redhead put her tiny feet on his hard dick. Sandy pulled his legs apart, She fondled his balls, squeezing them harder and harder. He was yelling between moans. She put her finger in her mouth then in his rectum. She found the sweet spot and began to move her finger in a circular motion. He screamed now. She pulled the lever to let the chair down. As it smashed the can, he exploded. It came out with such force that it hit her in the face and dribbled down her chest. He was panning, gasping for air, crying out, "Fucking fabulous!"

The petite redhead climbed down from her perch—it had gone soft.

Sandy grabbed a tissue from the counter and wiped her chest. Dr. Can Crusher said, "I have a special treat for you, girls."

He pulled out a tank of laughing gas and attached the mask. "This will make you feel really good." They took turns lying back in his chair, breathing in the mist. It didn't take long before they were all high. Slumped on the floor, the two girls crawled toward each other. Sandy kissed the redhead. The kiss was long and sweet. Red slid her hand down to one of Sandy's voluptuous breasts and started to suck.

"That feels so good," Sandy said. Sandy put her hand between Red's legs, rubbing her clitoris. The doctor lay in his chair, enjoying the show. High-pitched shrieks of joy filled the room. Simultaneous climaxes had left the two lying motionless on the floor.

At work the next day, Hope came in wearing a pair of sunglasses and slightly limping. Sandy wanted to ask what happened, but she already knew the answer. Don, her piece of shit boyfriend, not only liked rough sex, but he liked to hit and dominate. For the love of her, she couldn't understand why a beautiful woman like Hope would stay with such a creep. Hope didn't stay. She moved her customers to Sandy and some of the other girls. They were told to tell her clientele that she had been in a car accident. She wouldn't be back until next week. It ran through Sandy's mind, *I'd like to go over to her house and kick the crap out of that piece of slime, but it would only make things worse for her.*

The day was hectic, squeezing all of Hope's clientele in. She couldn't be late. She and Mr. X had plans to meet some of his friends at a local restaurant This would be the first time she would meet them. She glanced at her watch; she was already late. She hurried home as fast as she could. He was dressed and waiting. She didn't bother to take a bath. She put on a black lace dress and stilettos. She wanted to make a good impression.

"Go start the car. I'll be there in just a minute."

When the door shut, she grabbed one of her little helpers and took a swig out of the bottle of vodka and then hurried to the car.

"Why were you so late?"

"Hope was in a car accident, or so they say. She would be out of work the rest of the week. We had to squeeze her customers in to our schedule. You could have called."

"I'm sorry."

"Are you sure that's why you were late?"

"Why else would I be late? I know this was an important dinner, and I want to meet your friends."

He parked the car and gave her a look with squinted eyes. "I want you to be on your best behavior. No more than two drinks." She just nodded.

The hostess greeted them. "Your table will be ready in just a short while. The rest of your party is at the bar. The bar was full, but they found a table in the back. They ordered a round of martinis. Chatting back and forth, she didn't join in the conversation. There was no need. The guys were talking business, something she could care less about. She was in her own little world, daydreaming about what had happened the night before. She remembered that Dr. Can Crusher had given her a tiny sample. Excusing herself, she went to the ladies' room, fumbling in her purse, looking for it. She had put it in her change purse along with a piece of cut straw. She didn't bother to take it out of the little baggie. She stuck the straw in and inhaled hard. The bitter taste dripped down the back of her throat. It burned a little. Her sinus and throat were inflamed from doing all that cocaine the night before. As she got back to the table, everyone was standing, waiting for her. Their table was ready. Mr. X ordered a bottle of red wine. She would've rather had another martini, but anything would do to wash away the taste.

She thought she had been on her best behavior, but apparently Mr. X didn't think so. The ride home was dead silent. She knew how to push the right buttons. Entering the door, she grabbed him and pulled him close and kissed him. She led him to the bedroom and playfully pushed him onto the bed. She started very slowly to take her clothes off. She did a striptease, removing one piece at a time. She knew he couldn't resist that. Sliding onto the bed, she said, "You're not really mad at me." She started to undress him. She lightly bit his nipples—he really loved that. She kissing and licking his whole body, he was hard. She got on her hands and knees. He liked doggy style, and they hadn't done that in a while.

"Come on, big boy, do your thing."

When he was finished, he rolled over, taking her hands and kissing them. "Nobody can do what you do for me." He held her close. Everything had been forgiven and forgotten.

3

The alarm went off at seven. She had to be to work by eight thirty. She was not being late today. She had a full book and she was hungover. She wished she could call in sick but knew that was out of the question.

Just get through today, and then, freedom for two whole days, Sunday and Monday. Tuesday was her next scheduled day to work.

She had to go straight home after work, no stopping at the bar. She and Mr. X had a birthday party to go to for a colleague of his. It was his fiftieth surprise party being held at an exclusive restaurant in a private room. She wore a low-cut red dress and gold-strapped heels.

She waited for him. He was already an hour late. She called his office— no answer. She tried his cell—no answer. Worried something may have happened, she drove herself to the restaurant. The maître d' directed her to the private room. Mr. X and the rest of the party had already been seated and drinks had been served. There wasn't an empty chair. No place for her to sit. Mr. X looked up with surprise on his face. She gave him a confused look.

Leaning down, she whispered, "Maybe I'm not supposed to be here. You were to meet me more than an hour ago. They were all kidding me about being stood up and the mystery woman. I thought you were picking me up."

The waitress quickly made a seat for her. She smiled at the group. "Sorry, miscommunication," she said as she seated herself. She ordered a martini. After dinner, a large embellished cake with fifty burning candles was presented to him, and they all said, "Happy birthday and he's a jolly good fellow." It took him three tries to blow out the candles. Someone from the back yelled, "Don't forget to make your wish."

He replied, "Good friends like you, who needs wishes?"

One by one, the gifts were given. They were mostly stupid gag gifts—colored condoms, pink boxer shorts. Mr. X gave him a cane. The champagne flowed and the cake was cut. It was a multilayered chocolate, vanilla, and raspberry cake with a whipped-cream frosting.

Falling asleep on the way home, it seemed like only seconds that we were pulling into the driveway. Mr. X was unzipping her dress as she walked to the house. He grabbed her waist.

"I'm not over the hill, and I don't need a cane unless you want to spank me with it."

"I've really got a headache. All that champagne plus the martinis."

He said, "I can give you something that would make you forget all about your headache."

She held out her hands. "More please, and I hope it's not porridge."

It was the magic white pill with the blue top. She'd only done LSD once before. It brought out her innermost child, and that was a place she didn't mind visiting again. It was like Alice in Wonderland falling down the rabbit hole into a world of fantasy and make-believe. Everything turned to cartoon characters, and psychedelic flowers floated in the air. Mr. X was a large deer with huge antlers, and as he talked, music notes floated out of his mouth and flowers hung around his neck. She couldn't understand what he was saying. Every word was long and drawn out like a record being played on low speed. She danced around the room, drawing flowers in the air. As she wiggled her finger, they would shoot upward, leaving a trail like a comet. She would think of a color, and they would turn red, orange, pink, purple, cobalt blue, and magenta—which was her favorite.

They walked to the bed, taking off their clothes. Lying on her back, the ceiling was filled with stars. She could see the moon with all its rough surface and deep craters and dark spots. Mr. X mounted her. She could see their bodies melting together like a candle burning and the wax intertwining, flowing onto a plate, swirling together, making new patterns and colors. Her back arched. The room seemed to be filled with angels singing. It was her own voice crying out. The feeling was so strong that it felt like the stars in the heavens had imploded.

4

The weekend had been very hectic with lots of parties and lots of drinking. She felt like she would just like to have a nice evening with just her and Mr. X.

She would arrive home earlier than usual to surprise Mr. X, but he wasn't there. There wasn't a note or a phone call. That was so weird. He always arrived home before her. She called his cell, but there was no answer. She had a bad feeling in the pit of her stomach. This was so unlike him. Maybe he wanted to let her know how it felt to be late and left wondering when or if she would return. She had to admit it didn't feel good. She just couldn't figure it out. He was Mr. Reliable.

She drew a bath, putting scented beads into the water; his favorite was lilac. Then she dressed in the black leather cat suit and knee-high boots. With whip in hand, she would greet him at the door with a little love tap to his butt. She was sure that this would bring a smile to his face. She poured herself a tall drink. The hours ticked by. No Mr. X, no call. She couldn't imagine what had happened. Around midnight, the doorbell rang and woke her. She had fallen asleep still dressed in her costume. She yawned and rubbed her eyes and wondered why he would be ringing the doorbell. Opening the door, there stood two policemen.

"Do you live at this address?"

"Yes."

"A Mr. Lucas Warren was killed in a car accident earlier this evening. This was the address on his ID." She fell to her knees and began to weep. "Are you his wife?"

Through the tears, she simply said, "Girlfriend."

"We need to contact his next of kin. Do you know them and their address or phone number?"

"His parents are dead. He has a sister, but they haven't talked in years. I don't even know her name. He simply called her the bitch."

"Children?"

"He never married, and I don't know of any."

"How long have you been living at this address?"

"A little over a year. His associates could probably help you. They've worked together for years. I'm sure they know a lot more about his personal life than I do." She went to the desk and gave them one of his business cards.

One of the officers said, "We're sorry for your loss. We need your contact information, work phone number. I'm sure someone will be contacting you about what will happen next."

She poured herself a drink and drank it straight down. She poured another and made her way to the bedroom. She lay on the bed, sobbing so hard she could hardly breathe.

"What am I going to do now? I love him. I really loved him." She thought of all the things he had done for her that she had taken for granted. Now it was gone. No way to get it back. No one to turn to. No one who really cared. She drank the rest of her drink and fell into a drunken sleep.

When she woke, it was ten o'clock she reached for the phone to call work. There was no way she was going into work, not in her condition. The receptionist answered the phone. She asked to speak to Hope.

"Where are you?"

"I'm still at home." Hope could barely understand her. "Mr. X was killed last night in a car accident. I can't come in. I just can't think of what I'm going to do."

"I'm so sorry for you. I'll explain to them. It'll be okay. Should I come by after work?"

"I don't know. I just can't think. I'll call you later."

"I'm so sorry for you. I'm here if you need me."

She realized that she did have a good friend. As she hung up the phone, she fell back on the bed she wanted to kick and scream but didn't have the strength. She just lay there and sobbed. Minutes seemed like hours. Thoughts raced through her mind, most of them not making any sense. She had to go to the bathroom she crawled off the bed and onto the floor she was lightheaded and sick to her stomach. She crawled to the toilet and pulled herself up by the vanity. She was stiff in the costume. It was too much to try to take it off, so she just sat there and went.

What a mess I am. She remembered her mother's words. They rang in her head: "You make your bed, you lie in it." Now she wondered what bed would she be lying in.

She sat there for a long time. She could smell herself. It was a combination of cigarettes, alcohol, and urine. She managed to stand up and, with all the effort she could muster, pull off the costume. She left it in a pile on the floor. Looking at it, she thought, *That's me, just a big smelly pile of nothing.*

She made her way into the shower. The cold water running over her gave her a chill. Now that she was fully awake, she would have to face reality and deal with it. She wrapped a big bath towel around her. Pulling all the drawers out and opening all the cabinets, she looked to see what she could find. In the back of the closet, under a pile of towels, she felt a familiar shape—a pill bottle. Pulling it from the back, she could only hope that it would be what she had been looking for. Yes, she quickly opened it. For a moment, she thought about taking all of them. She poured them in her hand and looked at them. One by one, she put them back, leaving two. Putting them in her mouth, she turned the faucet on and cupped her hands, filling them with water. It was warm. She didn't care. She just needed something to help her swallow.

She went to the kitchen and made herself some coffee. She decided not to have a drink. She needed to be clearheaded. She knew that she wouldn't be able to stay there. Without him and not being his wife, she had no rights to anything. She walked through the house, looking to see if there would be anything she could take to pawn. She would need to have some money. She didn't find much, only a silver tea set that had been his mother's. Going to the bedroom, she opened his jewelry box. She knew she couldn't take it all. That would look suspicious. She looked at one piece at a time, deciding what she could take. There was a gold chain that a cross hung from. He didn't often wear it. He had mentioned that it was the last thing his mother had given him before she died. There were several pairs of gold cuff links and three watches. One was a Rolex with a gold nugget band. He only wore it on special occasions. It was the most valuable of all of them. She thought it would be a little risky to take it, but she was desperate.

She knew that he kept some cash on hand. She wondered where he kept it. She went to the closet and checked all the jacket pockets—nothing. He kept his best shoes in their boxes. One by one, she took them off the shelf.

Opening them, she felt inside, pushing her fingertips to the toes. The third pair, she hit pay dirt, pulling the roll of bills out. She counted it. It was more than she expected—$3,000.

She was still numb from the thought she would never see him again. She went to the bar in the living room and poured herself a drink and then another, pondering what to do next.

She got dressed then packed her clothes. She didn't want to be there when whoever came to tell her she would have to leave. She closed and locked the door behind her.

5

It was midday by now. She drove to work. Dave, the owner, was a real asshole womanizer and liar. She always dreaded having to speak to him face-to-face. She avoided it as much as possible.

"Sorry I didn't call this morning. I've just been beside myself. I hope you can forgive me." She knew buttering him up was the best tactic.

"I guess but you put us in a real bind. Under the circumstance, I won't fire you this time. Tomorrow you will be here?"

"Yes."

As she was leaving, Hope gave her a hug and a kiss on the cheek. "I didn't hear from you. I was worried."

"I'm okay. I just have a lot of things to work out. I'll see you tomorrow."

She drove to a cheap motel not far from work. It was $36 a night. Her money wouldn't last long at that rate. She'd have to think of something else, but for now it would do.

She didn't bother to unpack. She would just live out of her suitcases. She decided not to pawn the jewelry until later. She thought it would be safer that way. She could put it in her cabinet at work; it had a lock.

Later that day, she drove to Mr. X's office to see what his associates had found out. It was almost closing time. They were done for the day and just about ready to leave.

Looking at the receptionist, she said, "I'm Sandy, Mr. X's girlfriend." Tears filled her eyes.

The receptionist Barbra said, "Yes, I remember you."

"The police came to see me at the house the night he was killed. I couldn't tell them much, only his parents were dead and he had a sister but I didn't even know her name. Do you know anything?"

"They did contact us, but unfortunately, we didn't know anything either. Mr. X was a very private person."

Sandy wiped the tears that ran down her cheeks. "Yes, I know."

Barbara asked, "Are you still staying at the house?"

"No. It didn't feel right. I'm staying at a motel for right now. Do you know the name of his lawyer?"

Barbara was tapping her forehead with her finger, trying to remember. "Mr. Green, but I don't think he had a will. He always talked about getting one but he never got around to it."

"What happens if you die without a will and they can't find a living relative?"

"Your estate goes to the government I believe."

She put the keys to the house on the desk. "I won't be needing these." Walking to her car, she broke down. "I'm so sorry. I'm so sorry," she kept repeating, sobbing so hard she could barely breathe. She didn't know how long she had sat there.

Everyone had left the lot; it was empty. She felt empty, all alone, no one to really care about her now that Mr. X was dead. She thought of her mother. She had been in the institute for years. Sandy had only been there three times. She couldn't bear it. Now she wondered, was this the way her mother felt, that there wasn't anyone in the world that cared about her?

Sandy screamed, "Someone help me!" but like her mother, there was no one to hear her screams or to help her.

6

When she woke, she was hoping when she opened her eyes she'd be back in Mr. X's bed. The whole thing had been an awful nightmare, but reality hit her. Hopelessness washed over her like a wave, sending her into the abyss. She had the feeling of falling deeper and deeper into the unknown. It seemed as if her whole life was governed by events that kept her emotionally on edge.

For a moment, she didn't know where she was. Nothing seemed familiar. Sitting up in bed, she scanned the room. It was dark. The drapes were shut. Just a small beam of light shone through the crack where the curtains didn't meet.

Making herself get out of bed, she showered. The bathroom was disgusting. There was mold in the cracks of the tiles. It smelled as if no one had cleaned it for months. She thought, *One more step down and I would be homeless.*

It would be hard for her to go to work but she had no choice. The money that she had taken would only last a few weeks. She had no idea what the jewelry would bring. She wanted to keep it so she would have something to fall back on.

She would have to hurry. Being late for work would only make it worse. She was hoping to slip by David's room. She wasn't sure if she could control herself if he made any unkind remarks. He felt being the owner gave him the right to belittle his staff. His heart was made of stone. When his own wife died, he never gave his daughter anything of her mother's. He married that same year in the month of his anniversary. His daughter never fully recovered from her mother's death and the way her father had treated her.

7

It was the worst days at work she had ever had. She tried her best not to cry, but the sadness she felt was overwhelming. Leaning over doing a shampoo, mucus ran out of her nose. Her customer had her eyes closed. At the last second, she managed to catch it in her hand. Not really thinking, she just went back to shampooing.

She was like a robot doing one customer after another. She didn't know how she got through the day. No customers complained, so everything must have been okay. It was just a blur. She couldn't even remember who she did or what they had done.

Thank God for Hope. They walked outside, and Hope just put her arms around Sandy and held her close. Sandy could let all her emotions out. She began to sob. It felt good to have someone genuinely care about her. Hope's shoulder was wet with tears. Sandy's eyes were bloodred. At some point, her contacts must have come out and everything was a blur. Hope took her hand and led her into the bar.

"Let's go to the bathroom before ordering."

Sandy washed her face with cold water and blew her nose. Hope told her to blow it again. "Nothing can go up if something's coming down." She blew her nose so hard it made her ears pop. She got her glasses from her purse and put them on. She hated the way they looked. She closed the bathroom door behind her. Hope cut them two extra-large lines of cocaine. Hope did hers first and then Sandy. After Sandy rubbed her finger around, collecting the residue, she rubbed her gums with it. She looked at Hope.

"I hope you don't mind me doing that. It's like you said—it makes them numb like the rest of my body."

Hope gave her a hug. "I can't imagine how you got through the day. I haven't had a loved one die, but I knew how it feels to be numb. Every time Don hit me, my whole body went numb so I couldn't feel the pain." Now it was Sandy's turn to console Hope. They just stood there holding one another.

At the bar, they ordered their martinis and drank them in silence. Their tears and confessions unlocked a feeling that they had never had with another person.

At the bar several people that knew Sandy had heard of the tragedy. They were giving her their condolences. It was nice of them, but she didn't want to be reminded. She wanted to drink and do cocaine until it made her forget even if it was just for a little while.

Hope paid their bill and they walked outside. Hope suggested that they buy a bottle of tequila and go back to Sandy's place. Sandy hesitated. "I have to warn you that it's a real dump. It's all I can afford."

Hope squeezed her hand. "I don't care about that. It's only you I care about."

They walked to the liquor store and bought the most expensive bottle of tequila they had. Driving to the motel, they passed a roadside vegetable stand. They stopped and picked up some lemons. Sandy pointed to some little packets of salt left over from the last time she got a burger.

Sandy was right—the place was a dump. The carpets were stained and the air smelled of stale tobacco. Hope went back to the car and got the air freshener that hung from the mirror. They put it by the light on the nightstand. The warmth from the light made the fragrance more intense.

They both sat cross-legged on the bed. They didn't have a knife to cut the lemons. Sandy got a pair of scissors from her purse. They were very sharp. She cut through the lemon, and the scissors slipped, cutting her finger. The blood ran down her hand and onto the floor. Hope poured some tequila on the cut and got toilet paper and wrapped her finger. It was a deep cut. She had to change the paper several times. The bleeding stopped. Hope managed to cut the lemons in half. They sprinkle the salt onto them and took turns drinking from the bottle and sucking the sour, salty liquid in between.

When the bottle was empty, they lay back on the bed. Sandy rolled over and kissed Hope. She was surprised Hope kissed her back. Sandy grabbed her and said, "I need to feel alive." Neither of them hesitated. They both took off their clothes. Hope kissed Sandy's breast and then made her way down to her stomach. Neither of them had ever felt such passion with a woman. The memory of Mr. X faded into the background.

When they looked at the clock, it was nine. Hope was an hour late going home. She broke out in a sweat. She knew there'd be hell to pay. She'd been beaten for a lot less. Hope started to cry. Sandy put her arm around her.

"Don't worry. I'll go with you and explain."

Hope looked up at her. "You don't know Don like I do."

Sandy said, "You can tell him that you had a flat tire and a nice man in the parking lot helped you change it."

"Does that mean you won't be coming with me? He hit me so hard one time he broke two of my ribs. All because I told a waiter how wonderful the food was. He didn't even wait until we got home. He slammed me up against the car in the parking lot and began punching me. I passed out. He picked me up and threw me into the back seat. He drove me home. It was in December and the temperature had dropped to forty-five. I remember him leaning over me and saying, "You stay out here like a bad dog.' He put his face next to mine. 'I don't want to see you until morning.' I didn't have a blanket. I tried to curl up in a ball to keep warm. My broken ribs were so painful that I couldn't. I had to lie there all night, stretched out flat and shivering."

Sandy kissed her and said, "Why go back? Just stay here with me. He doesn't know where to look for you."

"He will in the morning when we have to go back to work. I know him. He'll tear through the shop, kicking anybody out of his way that is in his path. If he doesn't kill me, Dave will surely fire me."

Sandy looked into her eyes. "I won't let him hurt you."

"Exactly what could you do?"

Sandy said, "He's only five feet eight inches and weighs about 160 pounds. I think I could take him on."

Hope looked at her. "He's all muscle and he packs a mean punch."

Sandy put her arm around. "Hope, we will call the police and get a restraining order."

Hope took Sandy's arm from around her. "I tried that once before. When he was served, he came right back over and put me in the hospital. I told them I was riding my bike and hit a curb. I was thrown over the handle bars. I know they didn't believe me, but I didn't change my story. Don told me the next time it wouldn't be the hospital. It would be the graveyard."

"We could let air out of one of your tires and you couldn't get the lug nuts off. We couldn't find anyone to help us. That's why you were late and why I had to bring you home."

Hopes knees were knocking. She was so nervous. "You have to let me go up first and try to explain."

Sandy said OK.

When they got to the apartment, Don was standing in the doorway. Hope had a gut feeling that this story was not going to work. He had a beer in his hand, and by his stance, she could tell he was drunk. Sandy took Hope's keys from her.

"Once you're inside, go to the living room. I can see you through the window. If it looks like you're in trouble, I'll be able to let myself in."

Hope said, "He might be drunk, but once he gets me inside, believe me he'll lock the door so I can't get out."

Hope walked toward the apartment. She was already trying to explain to him why she was late. "I had a flat tire and I couldn't find anyone to help me. I couldn't get the lug nuts off. One of the girls from the shop stayed with me, and when we realized how late it was getting, she drove me home."

Don started yelling, "Liar! Liar! Liar!"

Hope took a step back. "What do you mean?"

"I went by the shop. My boss let me off early. I was going to take you out for a drink. Your car was in the parking lot, but it didn't have a flat tire. I looked all over for you, but you weren't there." He stepped toward her and grabbed her by the shoulder. He dragged her into the apartment. He shut and locked the door. Hope managed to break free and run to the living room. Sandy could see she was in real trouble. Taking the scissors out of her purse, she ran to the apartment, opening the door with Hope's keys. She saw him dragging her by her throat to the kitchen. He was choking her. Her lips were blue. Without thinking of the consequences, Sandy plunged the scissors into the back of his neck. She had severed his spinal cord. He was dead in seconds. She pulled him off Hope. She wasn't moving. Sandy tilted her head back and pinched her nose. She blew as hard as she could into her mouth. Then she did it again. She put her hands on Hope's chest and started pumping—1, 2, 3, 4, 5, 6, then she blew another breath into her lungs. Hope began to cough. Sandy grabbed her and held her close.

"You're alive. I thought I lost you." She cupped Hope's face with her hands and kissed her forehead.

Hope looked over at Don. "Is he dead?"

"I think so. He hasn't moved."

Hope couldn't believe it. "What are we going to do? Should we call the police?"

Sandy sat on the floor next to him. "I don't know—let me think." Her thoughts were splintered. "We could call the police or get rid of the body or leave it here and make it look like a break-in. I think we need to get rid of the body."

Hope was still recovering from being choked. "Why not call the police and just explain?"

"How do we explain that I had a pair of scissors in my hands? The story would go, I brought you home. I saw him choking you. I just happen to have your keys and a pair of scissors in my hand and stabbed him to death. I've been on two juries, and believe me, the people that they pick always seem to want to find the person guilty. I just can't take that chance."

"People saw us together at the bar and at the liquor store. The owner of the motel was outside when we pulled up. He saw us go in together."

"Detectives have a way of breaking you down. If they found out we were lovers, it would look premeditated. If we get rid of the body, you can say you got into an argument. And that you stayed the night here with me. He had gotten violent with you in the past. You were afraid to go back. You told me that he wasn't close to any of his family. He didn't keep in contact with them. They won't be looking for him. His boss knows he drinks, and sometimes, he just doesn't come in to work. He doesn't even call. He just shows up. This time he just doesn't come back. I don't think his boss would put in a missing-person's report."

Sandy picked up his feet and told Hope to help her put him in the bathtub. Then go put on some of his old clothes and a baseball cap. "Pull the cap down so your face can't be seen. Then go get ice from the ice machine. Look around. I don't think they have any cameras in the hallways."

Hope put on the clothes and got a plain baseball cap and pulled it down so her face couldn't be seen. Sandy started to clean up the blood. It was a tile floor so that made it easier. She scrubbed. it with soapy bleach water. Then she went to the bathroom and got fingernail polish remover. She thought that this would take any remaining bloodstains that she may have left.

Hope came back. "There weren't any cameras in the hallways. As far as I can tell, there's only one camera. It views the parking lot. How are we going to get the body to the car?"

Sandy put her hand on Hope's shoulder. "We're going to put them in the back of his truck. You being dressed in his clothes from a distance, will look like him."

Sandy asked if Don had any of his work tools there. Hope pointed to the closet by the door. "He kept a few in there." Sandy looked through them. She found a hacksaw.

Hope hung her head down. "I can't help you." She ran to the sink and threw up. "Just thinking about it makes me sick."

Sandy walked over to her. "I'll do it, but you will have to help me carry him out. I'll put it in trash bags so you don't have to see."

"I'm going to need a couple of stiff drinks and a big line of cocaine." Hope poured them both a glass of vodka. She went to the bedroom and brought out an eight ball of cocaine. Don did a little drug selling to offset the cost of their habit. Sandy drank the vodka without even taking a breath. Hope made two lines on the kitchen counter. After they snorted them, Sandy wanted another vodka. Hope looked at her. "You want to get even drunker and high and may be get stopped by the cops? Let's just get this over with."

Sandy went into the bathroom with the hacksaw. Hope sat outside the door. Sandy left the bags in the tub. When the job was done, she took down the plastic shower curtain. She scrubbed the tub and the walls and then sprayed them with mildew remover. If it could remove mold, she was hoping it could remove blood.

The two of them carried the curtain into the living room. Dressed in Don's clothes, Hope drove the truck to an empty parking space close to the apartment. Sandy passed the bags to her. She carried them to the truck. When they were done, Hope followed Sandy through the back roads out of town. Twenty miles down the road, Sandy found a gravel road that ran alongside of the railroad track. They followed the tracks about four miles and came across a thickly wooded area. By now, it was midnight.

Sandy saw what she thought was a path. She pulled the car a little past it. That made the truck stop right in front of the trail. She told Hope to move over and let her drive. She backed the truck up on the bank of the tracks and pulled forward. With the headlights on, she was right. They'd found an old hunting trail. It didn't look like it'd been used in a very long time. The weeds were three feet high, and the actual path was covered with debris from storms.

Sandy told Hope, "Go get the car and back it up. I'm going to try to make a U-turn so the bed of the truck lines up with the pathway. Once I've done that, pull the curtain back of me so we can use the lights to see."

After rearranging the vehicles, she stopped and put the tailgate down. They got out of the vehicles. They each took an end of the shower curtain and carried it into the woods. It was heavy, and they couldn't carry it too far. Sandy saw slight depression by the side of the trail.

"This looks like it'll have to be the spot." They had forgotten to bring a shovel. They were determined to bury him even if they had to dig the hole with their hands.

They sat on the ground one on one side of the burial spot and one on the other. Sandy looked over at Hope.

"Dig as if your life depends on it because it does."

Their fancy nails and polish didn't last long. Hope looked down at her broken nail.

"You need to find it. Have you ever heard of DNA? Go back to the car and get the scissors. We need to cut your nails short. One little sliver could find and identify us." Hope made her way to the car and got the scissors. She thought she saw a faint light down the track. She ran back down the path as fast as she could. She was out of breath by the time she reached Sandy.

"I think I see the train coming."

They love what they were doing and ran back to the vehicles. There was no time. The light was getting closer.

"We have to back farther down the trail so we can't be seen." They had turned their lights off just in time before the train passed.

They walked back to the burial site. The ground was soft and dry. It was still difficult to dig with their hands but not impossible. It took more than two hours for them to dig the hole deep enough. They dropped the body parts in the curtain in the hole. Then they put the dry pine needles and pinecones that they had gathered into the hole and lit it on fire. The curtain and bags melted, destroying any fingerprints that they may have left behind. They were exhausted. Lying on the ground, they used their feet and legs to push the pile of dirt back into the hole. They gathered leaves and sticks and put them over the grave to camouflage it.

By the time they got back to Sandy's, it was six o'clock in the morning. They had to be at work at eight thirty. Both girls got in the shower together. It was a tight squeeze. One scrubbed the top, the other scrubbed the bottom and then they reversed it. There wasn't any soap. Sandy had taken a bottle of shampoo from work. It made so many bubbles that it ran onto the bathroom floor. After drying all, she threw the towel on the wet floor.

"What are you waiting for? Get the white stuff out and I'll roll a dollar up."

Both of them had done two big lines. Their nerves were on edge and they were cranked. Their adrenaline was pumping. Hope looked at Sandy. "I don't know if that was such a good idea. I feel weird."

Sandy was helping Hope to the bed, but she collapsed on the floor. Her eyes rolled back, and her body became rigid. She was having a seizure. Everything that had happened that day and night had overwhelmed her to the point of total exhaustion. Doing the lines of cocaine was just too much for her system. Sandy took her cell phone from her pocket and called 911.

She could hear the sirens of the ambulance coming. She took the rest of the cocaine and wiped the counter and flushed it down the toilet. They put their bloodied clothes in a garbage bag. She ran and put them in the dumpster outside. The garbage would be picked up in the morning.

The ambulance pulled up. The door was open. Two men and a woman carrying equipment rushed in. One of the men leaned down to try to find a pulse. He said, "I found one. She's alive." He quickly gave her oxygen and inserted a needle to hydrate her. They put her on a gurney and loaded her into the back of the ambulance. Sandy asked if she could come with them. She was told to follow them in her car to the hospital.

When they reached the hospital, she could hear one of the men yelling, "Code blue! Code blue!"

She tried to follow them into the emergency room but she was told to go to the registration counter. When she got there, they wanted to know the patient's full name.

"Hope Epps."

"Does she have any insurance?" Sandy said she didn't know. "What about her address?"

"I don't know that either."

The woman behind the counter asked if she was a relative. Sandy said, "Yes, her sister."

The woman behind the counter said, "It's awfully strange that you don't even know where your own sister lives." She told her to go to the waiting room and someone would let her know what was happening. She knew that if she told them that they were just friends they wouldn't be able to tell her anything because of the confidentiality protocol.

She was still high from the cocaine that she had done earlier. She felt like she was going to jump out of her skin. Two policemen were walking toward her.

"Are you the patient's sister?"

She hesitated and then said yes. She knew they were going to ask her if her sister had been doing drugs. She was shaking inside but tried her best to keep her composure. One of the policemen put his hand on her shoulder.

"We have bad news. Your sister passed away. We think it's from an overdose."

Sandy was stunned. She couldn't move. Her eyes filled with tears. She couldn't breathe. She felt like she was going to pass out. She couldn't believe after all she and Hope had done to save her from a monster, she was dead. Sandy could barely stand up. One of the officers helped her to her feet. She told him she needed to go to the bathroom. He walked her down the hallway and waited outside. She washed her face with cold water. Fear hit her like a wave and knocked her to the floor. She threw up. She could hear a knocking at the door.

"Are you okay?"

She couldn't answer. Now there was pounding on the door.

"Are you okay?

She had passed out. The next thing she remembered there were several people picking her up and putting her into a wheelchair. They took her to the emergency room and removed her clothes and put her into a hospital gown. They put her clothes in a big plastic bag then put her in bed. A nurse said, "A doctor will be with you shortly." Meanwhile, the officer stood outside the door.

A nurse came in to draw her blood. "Can you do that without my permission, or can I refuse?" The officer stepped inside. She looked at him. "Am I under arrest?"

He walked to the side of the bed. "No, but we do want to ask you about the events that led up to your sister's death."

"Does that mean that you can't keep me here?" She got out of bed and told them she was going to leave.

The officer said, "You can leave, but we will be taking you down town to the station for questioning."

Looking at the nurse, Sandy said, "Bring me my clothes."

The officer shook his head. "No, we will be keeping them, along with your sister's until we determine what caused her death."

Sandy looked quite puzzled. "Then what am I going to wear?"

The nurse brought in another hospital gown and said, "She could put this one on backward. That way you will be covered."

Sandy just looked at the officer. "This is ridiculous. I can't go down to the station in this. I have to go back to my place and put on some clothes. Then come down to the station."

"One of the officers will follow you. Meanwhile, we have had a forensic team in the motel looking for any kind of evidence that may help us in solving your sister's death."

"How do you know where I live?"

"The ambulance report."

Driving home, Sandy was going over and over in her mind how well they had cleaned up. They were probably just looking for drugs. She did have a few Valium and a couple of black beauties underneath her clothes in the bottom of her suitcase. By the time they got back to the motel, everyone had left. The officer followed her inside. She went through her suitcase looking for something to wear but also checking if they had found the bottle. It was missing. She got a pair of jeans and a blouse and went into the bathroom to change.

8

When they walked outside, to Sandy's surprise, he put her in the back seat of the cruiser.

"I thought you told me I wasn't under arrest."

As the officer shut the door, he said, "You're not."

"Then why can't I take my own car? How will I get back to the motel?" He assured her that they would bring her back. Her head was spinning. She was coming down from her high. She had so many mixed emotions. She couldn't believe after all she and Hope had done to set her free from a monster, Hope was dead. Sandy wondered if this could be karma coming back to bite her in the ass.

When they got to the police station, they pulled around the back. Metal gates opened and they drove in. Opening the back door of the cruiser, he told Sandy to follow him. They entered a hallway that led to a waiting room. It was filled with all kinds of people—young, old, black, white, women that looked like they worked the streets. He told Sandy to sit down and that someone would come and get her when they were ready. Looking around the room, she couldn't help but wonder how many other murderers were sitting among them.

Sandy was really coming down hard. She was sweating and her head was pounding. Her mouth was dry. Her tongue stuck to the roof of her mouth. She wanted some water, but there didn't seem to be anyone to ask.

A woman officer came to where Sandy was sitting. She told her to come with her. They went inside a small room. It did look like the interrogation rooms that she had seen on television. Sandy asked the woman if she could have a drink of water. The officer left, and in a short while, two male officers came in. One was carrying a bottle of water. He handed the bottle to her, and she quickly opened it and drank half.

He introduced himself, "I'm Officer Brown." He sat down across from her and Officer Jones stood by the door. Officer Brown asked her if she was feeling okay. Sandy's forehead was all sweaty. It was running down her face and into her eyes, making them sting. The officer by the door left and came back with a box of tissues. She took several and blotted her forehead and wiped her eyes.

Officer Brown said, "So you and your sister were doing drugs earlier?"

Sandy looked at him right in his eyes. "I have to tell you something. Hope isn't my sister. I just told them that at the hospital so they would let me know what was going on."

Brown asked, "Do you know if she has any relatives?"

"We were friends and worked together at a place called Dave's Curls and Locks. Hope had only worked there three months. She never talked about her family."

The two officer changed places. Jones put Hope's driver's license on the table. It was issued in Nebraska and would have expired next month. Sandy took another drink of water.

"Maybe she was waiting until then to renew it. Like I said, she never talked about her family."

"Where did she live?"

Sandy wiped her brow. "I don't know."

The officer leaned forward. "You mean you worked together for three months and she never told you where she lived?"

"That's right. She said she had a jealous boyfriend that didn't allow her to bring anyone over."

"Do you know his name?"

"Not really, she just called him asshole. She didn't like to talk about him because she said it ruined a good time." Sandy leaned back in her chair. "We went out for drinks after work. She told me that her boyfriend dealt drugs, mostly cocaine. She would occasionally bring some and share it with me. I never bought any. It's not like I did it every day, just when we got together for a few drinks after work. We blow off a little steam and share stories about our customers before heading home. My boyfriend was killed in a car accident not too long ago. I'm still not over it, and Hope was a good shoulder to cry on."

The officer placed the bottle that they had found in her suitcase on the table along with some bloodied tissue paper.

"I thought you said you didn't buy drugs?"

"I don't."

"Where did you get these from?"

"Friends. I really don't remember who gave them to me."

"What about the bloodied tissue?"

"I cut my finger trying to slice the lemons in half." She held out her finger so they could see the cut.

"Having those in your possession is a felony." Officer Brown told Sandy to stand up and they placed her under arrest for having a controlled substance. After they read her rights to her, they handcuffed her.

"It is good for you that the state of Florida has a Good Samaritan law. Because you called for an ambulance to try to save Hope's life, you won't be charged with manslaughter." They took her to the booking area. They fingerprinted her and took mug shots. Sandy had never been in trouble before. She never had her fingerprints taken. Now they would be on file. She hoped that she had cleaned up all her prints from Hope's apartment. She knew the police would be going to the shop to ask questions about Hope. She didn't know if Hope was at that address when she started work.

Hope did mention that they had only been in the apartment for about six weeks. Sandy didn't know where she had lived before that. She probably didn't mention the move to Dave. Nobody wanted to talk to him unless it was absolutely necessary. He always had the W-2 forms mailed to the shop and they got our paychecks at work on Friday. She was pretty sure he would only have her old address. Don was such a control freak. He handled all the money that the utilities would be in his name.

After they were finished booking Sandy, she asked to go to the bathroom. A lady officer walked with her and waited outside the door. She was so overwhelmed she broke down. Sitting on the floor, she started screaming, "Someone help me!"

The officer opened the door and helped her off the floor. "You get a phone call. Is there someone you can call?"

Sandy just shook her head no. They put her in a holding cell that had several other women in it. She was so confused by the events of the last few weeks especially the last twenty-four hours that joining Hope didn't seem like such a bad idea.

Sandy sat on one of the benches with her eyes closed. She had no idea what would happen next. One of the other women came and sat down by her, asking, "What are you in for?"

Sandy opened her eyes and saw a middle-aged woman that had a miniskirt and a tube top on. Sandy told the woman, "Possession of a controlled substance."

The woman introduced herself, "I'm Jean."

"I'm Sandy." Then she asked, What are you in for? Prostitution, Sandy's mouth almost flew open. She couldn't believe that a man would pay to have sex with such an unattractive middle-aged woman. Sandy asked Jean, "How much do you get per customer?"

Jean smiled. Her teeth were stained and several were missing. "It depends on what they want—fifteen dollars for a hand job, twenty-five dollars for a blow, and thirty-five dollars for the full package."

Sandy could not believe she got more for a haircut than Jean got for a blow job.

Sandy closed her eyes again. "This is a nightmare. I've never been in jail before." Sandy asked, "What happens next?"

Jean had been arrested multiple times. She told her, "You'll get bail hearing sometime tomorrow. How much did they catch you with?"

"Only three Valium and two black beauties."

Jean patted Sandy on the back. "You've got nothing to worry about. They will let you out on your own recognizance. That means you won't have to put up any money or get a bail's bondsman. For that small of an offense, you will probably only get probation."

Jean sat down on one of the benches and told Sandy, "You might as well lay down and try to get some sleep. It's going to be a long night."

9

The next morning Sandy felt like a Mack truck had hit her. She had gotten very little sleep. Every time she closed her eyes, she would replay the events of the last forty-eight hours. It was more than a nightmare. It's as if she had stepped out of her body and she was watching this other person that looked like her do the unspeakable actions.

"Hi, it's Rose. Remembered me? I'm the one telling the story. I told you that I would try to be the voice of reason. I might have been born frail and weak, but tucked away in Sandy's brain over the years, I have become much stronger. I decided that we need to get rid of the body. I was the one who gave Sandy the strength to do what she had to done. We didn't want to go to jail or, even worse, prison for the rest of our lives."

Jean was still sleeping. Sandy wanted to wake her up so she would have someone to talk to. She wanted a distraction to stop her brain from playing over and over again all that had happened. It was driving her crazy. An officer came to get Sandy and the other women. He was taking them to their arraignment. They followed him down a corridor to a courtroom. They were told to sit and that a public defender would come in and talk to them about how they would plea. A nice-looking man in his thirties came in carrying a briefcase. Sandy was first on his list to talk to.

He introduced himself, "I'm Mr. Hargreaves." Then he started to explain she would be called by her case, number 321. He asked Sandy how did she want to plea.

She looked at him and asked, "How should I plea?"

He fumbled through his papers, finding her case. "This is your first offense, and you were caught with such a small amount. I would plead guilty. You will probably only get probation."

When they had finished talking, he moved down the line, talking with each of the other women. The judge came in, and everyone stood up. Once the judge was seated, the bailiff said, "You can be seated." When her number was called, the judge asked her how she plead.

With her attorney, Mr. Hargreaves, by her side, Sandy said, "Guilty."

The judge looked at her. "Because this is your first offense, you will be released on your own recognizance. Your next hearing will be in two weeks."

Sandy looked at her attorney. "Does that mean I can go? I'm not going back to jail?"

"That's correct, but you must show up in two weeks. I will meet you here at the courthouse a couple of hours before your sentencing. I think I can work out a deal that you will only get probation. One of the conditions of being on probation is that you have a job. Do you have one?"

Sandy said, "I did, but I don't think I have one anymore."

The attorney made it perfectly clear that between now and the time they went back to court, it was imperative that she had a job. Sandy was so elated she was free that she put her arms around the attorney and gave him a hug.

An officer escorted Sandy back down the hallway to an area that had a counter. She was told to sit until her name was called. When Sandy's name was called, a woman officer gave her a bag that had her belongings, which they had taken when she was booked—her purse, belts, a bracelet, and a ring.

Sandy looked at the officer that had escorted her there. "When I was brought here for questioning, I didn't think I would be arrested. The officer that assured me said he would take me back to the motel. So how do I get there?"

The two officers looked at each other and shrugged their shoulders. The male officer said, "We're not a taxicab, lady. It's up to you to find your own way home."

Sandy took the bag off the counter. She put her belt on and then her ring and bracelet She threw her pocketbook over her shoulder. As she was leaving she mumbled that cops were all liars.

Walking outside, Sandy realized that being free to go not having to answer to anyone was one of the greatest feelings she had ever felt. She looked in her purse. She only had twenty-five dollars, and she didn't want to spend it on a cab. The motel was six miles from the police station. It felt so good to be outside she decided she would walk. She remembered that her grandmother whistled while she worked. She always said it makes the time go by faster, and before you know it, your chores were done. She had loved her grandmother so that it was one of the greatest losses in her life when she died. She found herself whistling a familiar tune that she had heard her grandmother whistle. It seemed like no time at all when she reached the motel. The door was unlocked. She remembered in all the confusion she must have forgotten to lock it. The keys were still on the nightstand. She lay down on the bed and tried to think of what she was going to do next.

Hope and she had left the truck in the woods. They had planned to go back the next day after work. They would have talked it over and decided what they were going to do with it Now it would be up to her to decide how she would get there. Sandy decided she would drive her car partway and hike the rest then take the truck to another location and burn it. She knew from her ex-husband, a mechanic, that cars were identified by their VIN number. She didn't know how at that moment she would destroy it. She would figure it out before she went. If the police found the truck, there wouldn't be any reason to connect her to it. With all that was going on, she still had to find a job.

When she called the shop, David told her she was fired. She could come and pick up her stuff after work when the shop was closed. He would wait for her. All the stations had a locked cabinet where the stylist kept their equipment in. Sandy was glad that she had left the remaining pain pills that she had taken from Mr. X's office there. If she had them in her suitcase, she would be in a lot more trouble. She drove to the shop that evening to collect her stuff and leave the key. David didn't want to lose her clientele. He told her that her clients knew she had been arrested for drugs. She didn't want to start over at a new shop. She didn't want to be the new girl. She had learned from the past being a low woman on the totem pole at a new shop was hell. That's why she had been so nice and friendly to Hope. Now the question was, where could she hide the pills? She didn't want to get rid of them because she didn't know how she would be able to get any more. She went back to the motel and took two. There was a small flower bed outside her window, so she buried them there. It was late. No one was in the parking lot. She was sure no one had seen her.

The next morning, she went out and got a newspaper. Looking through the Wanted ads, she saw a job opening at a restaurant nearby. She had been a waitress before she had become a hairstylist. She got dressed and drove to the restaurant. It was called the Tick Tack. They specialized in breakfast and it was open twenty-four hours a day.

The restaurant was nicely decorated. It was bright and cheerful. She asked the cashier who would she see about getting an application for a job. The cashier directed her to the back of the restaurant.

"Go through a door that says Employees Only. The manager's office is on the left."

She knocked and a male voice told her to come in. A gray-haired man was sitting behind a desk. He looked up.

"May I help you?"

Sandy told him that she wanted an application to apply for the job that she had seen in the paper. The gray-haired man stood up and introduced himself.

"I'm Mr. Brady, the manager."

As she sat down, she told him that she was Sandy Nash. He got an application out of a desk drawer. He asked her if she had any experience. Sandy told him that she had been a waitress, but that it had been a few years back. Mr. Brady asked her what kind of work she had been doing. She didn't want to tell him about how she lost her job. Instead she told him that she had been caring for her sick mother and that she had recently passed away.

"When my mother died, she was in heavy debt. The bank was foreclosing on my mother's house." That she only had weeks to move and that she desperately needed the job. Her story must have touched his heart because he smiled at her and said, "You're hired." Then he asked, "Can you start tomorrow?" Sandy told him if he needed her, she could start that afternoon. Mr. Brady said that he had enough girls scheduled for that day, but tomorrow morning, she should come in by eight o'clock and she should wear a white blouse and black pants.

Sandy felt relieved that she had found a job. There was still the question of what she was going to do with the truck. She decided that she would get rid of it that night She wanted to start her new job not having to worry about it.

By the time she got home, it was one o'clock. She changed into a pair of jeans and a black hooded sweat jacket. She drove her car to the closest little town to where they had left the truck. She parked in the back of a small strip mall. She walked to the highway. She was walking when she heard a horn blow. There was a man in an old beat-up Ford Ranger. She walked to the passenger side of the truck. The man had rolled down the window. He asked her if she needed a ride and how far she was going.

"About six miles my car broke down. I was on my way to see my aunt." When they came to a small subdivision, Sandy told him that he could let her out there. Her aunt lived a couple of streets down. She could walk the rest of the way. She started walking in the direction of the houses. When she was sure that the truck was out of sight, she turned around and walked back to the highway. She pulled the hood of the sweatshirt up to cover her hair. She was walking looking down so you couldn't see her face. When she reached the railroad, she ran as fast as she could to the truck. She drove it back to the highway. Most of the land between the two towns were undeveloped forest. She had decided not to burn the truck but just take the tag and the VIN off. They wouldn't be able to find the owner. She turned off the highway and drove the truck into the woods and left it. She walked back through the woods a good distance before going back to the highway.

Walking back, she was so deep in thought that she didn't realize she was walking in the road. She heard a horn blow and then tires squealing. When she turned around, a car had stopped just feet from her. A lady with a child in the back seat was screaming at her, "Are you an idiot! You walked right off the side of the road into my path. I could have killed you. What were you thinking?"

Sandy didn't know what to say. She didn't want to look up so the woman could see her face. She just kept staring at the ground and said, "I'm sorry." The lady yelled "stupid" as she drove off.

By the time Sandy had gotten back to her car, she was exhausted and starving. She decided to wait until she got back to Dunedin before stopping and getting something to eat. She went to the Wolves Den Inn. It was a bar and a quaint little restaurant. She knew the bartender, Danny. If, for any reason someone asked her where she had been, she could use this as an alibi. She ordered chicken wings and a vodka on the rocks.

Danny asked her where she had been. He hadn't seen her in a while. Sandy drank the vodka and ordered another.

"My boyfriend was killed in a car accident so I had to move. I was so overcome with grief I couldn't go to work. My boss fired me. I had to move to a ratty motel and find a new job."

Danny brought her drink and said, "Boy, you've really had a run of bad luck. The drinks are on me."

She had known Danny for quite a while. She knew that he had done cocaine. She had gotten really drunk at the bar one night and had stayed until closing. After everyone else had left and the bar was closed, Danny asked her if she'd like to do a couple of lines of cocaine with him. She jumped at the chance. After, they had sex on the pool table. It'd been a onetime thing, but she hoped history would repeat itself.

10

She was in the middle of eating her chicken wings when Danny gave her another vodka on the rocks. "This is your last freebie."

Sandy looked up at him. "What about a repeat, you know the night I stayed after the bar closed?"

Danny told her that he met a wonderful woman that changed his life. "I'm on the straight and narrow. It sounds like you should do a little soul- searching yourself. I know the road you're going down can only lead to self-destitution."

Sandy drove back to the motel. She wanted to bury her other bottle of pills. It made her nervous to have them with her. It was still light and people were in the parking lot. She was buzzed from the vodka. She took two of the pills she had gotten from the shop. She decided to take a little nap. When she woke, it was dark outside. She had slept for almost four hours. She took two more pills out of the bottle and then walked outside and looked around.

She didn't see anybody, so she quickly dug where the other bottle had been buried. She put the other bottle in the hole then buried them again. The pills helped her to relax and sleep, but she was still craving the high that cocaine gave her. Now that Hope was gone, the only person she knew that had some was Dr. Can Crusher, but for now, she would have to put those thoughts on the back burner. She set her alarm clock for 6:00 a.m. She wanted to go back to sleep, and when she would wake up in the morning, it would be a new day and a new start.

When the alarm went off, she got up and took a bath and dressed. She wore a white blouse that buttoned up the front. She left the first four buttons open so you could just see a little cleavage. The black pants fit her like a glove. She was looking forward to her new job. When she arrived, the floor manager Mary introduced her to the other servers. They had just changed shifts. She would work from eight to four. It was like riding a bike—she got right back into the hang of it. She noticed that the majority of people in the restaurant were men. That suited her just fine. She unbuttoned one more button of her blouse. She was friendly and had a great smile. That worked wonders. The smallest tip she got all day was a dollar for a cup of coffee. When her shift was over, she really didn't want to go back to the motel. She asked Mary if she needed any extra help on the next shift. They worked four to midnight.

"One of the girls did call in sick. Are you sure that you won't get too tired?"

Sandy told Mary that she really needed the money. She was used to not getting much sleep, caring for her elderly mother. Mary pointed to the back booth and told her to eat something. The restaurant didn't get busy until around five o'clock. Her hands were shaking a little bit. It had been nine hours since she had a drink. She had put a bottle of vodka in her trunk. She walked to her car and got the bottle. She squatted down so no one could see her and took several big swallows. It didn't take long before her hands stopped shaking. She went back into the restaurant and sat in the back booth, ordering a ham-and-cheese sandwich and a Coke.

As she was eating, her thoughts drifted back to all that had happened. She could still remember the smell of Mr. X. It was heavenly. Better than any perfume she had ever had. The memory of Hope's beautiful face and her friendly smile made a tear come to her eye. She had truly loved them both. She realized she knew what love felt like. Lost in her memories, the hour past quickly. It was time to go back to work.

Most of the tables were families. She buttoned her blouse and started her second shift. The tables that had children at them she made sure she commented on how cute they were or how well-behaved. Just this little bit of extra effort helped her get a bigger tip. She had to admit that she liked the morning shift much better. She counted her tips. She had made almost twice as much in the morning. She was grateful for all the money she had made that day. It meant for now she would have a place to lay her head at night.

11

When she got back to the motel, her feet and legs were killing her. She had done ten hours at the beauty shop before, and they only hurt a little. She realized sixteen hours was too much for her. She fell into bed in her work clothes and fell fast asleep. She didn't wake up until seven. She had to be to work by eight. She felt awful. Her hands were shaking so bad it was hard to get the vodka bottle to hold still long enough to take a drink from it. After three or four swallows, she washed her face and brushed her teeth. She didn't have time for a bath. Her clothes were not too wrinkled so she didn't change them. Her hair was a mess. She pulled it back in a ponytail. Putting on a little blush and lipstick, she headed for work. She arrived five minutes early.

The restaurant was packed. Looking around the room, she already recognized a few faces. They were the ones that had left her the biggest tip. She was assigned a section of tables, and unfortunately, none of them were sitting in her area. A man named Wayne stopped her as she walked by.

"I missed you this morning. I guess I came in a little too early."

She smiled. "I guess you did. I don't start work till eight."

He gave her a five-dollar bill. "That's for your smile. It has brightened my day. Tomorrow I won't get here until after eight. When you see me, point to where I should sit."

She patted him on the back. "I'll make sure I do that."

At noon, Mary pulled her aside and asked if she wanted to work a double shift. Sandy told her, "You were right. Sixteen hours on my feet was too much. I was exhausted by the time I got home. If you need a little extra help, I could work four hours more, but sixteen is just too much."

Mary said, "I'll keep that in mind."

Sandy thought she might as well let Mary know that she would have to have Thursday off. That was when she was due in court. She told Mary that she had just heard that there were a few loose ends about her mother's estate.

"Thursday was the only time the law could see me. I just found out yesterday. I really don't want to take off from work. I need the money. I am only child, and there's no one else that can do this. My father's dead."

Mary said, "Of course you can have off. Sometimes, things come up that we have to tend to."

The restaurant was busy the whole time she was there. When her shift was over, she went to the back booth and counted her tips. Not as much as the day before, but it was still enough for her to get by on. She took the five-dollar bill out of her other pocket that Wayne had given her. He had a wedding band on. He was another one of those jerks that cheated on his wife. Too bad he was married. For a middle-aged man he was really handsome.

She drove back to the motel. She poured herself a vodka on the rocks and lay on the bed and drank it. She was really craving one of her little helpers, but it was still light out. She hadn't eaten all day. She could have gotten something from the restaurant, but she was in a hurry to get home and have a drink. The bottle in the trunk was empty. There was a little home-style restaurant around the corner from the motel. It was a real greasy spoon, but it was the closest place to get something to eat.

When she walked in, she almost walked out. It was dark inside and had a funny smell. Her stomach was growling—she was so hungry. She decided to stay. The waitress came by and threw the menu on the table. Looking through the menu, Sandy decided, *What would be the safest thing to eat in a place like this? A grilled cheese and a Coke, they can't hardly mess that up.*

It was a while before the waitress came back, and Sandy couldn't help but be a little annoyed. She placed her order, and it was twenty minutes before the waitress came back with her food. Sandy thought, *I bet this bitch doesn't make good tips. She certainly isn't going to get one from me. I'll never come back to this place no matter how hungry I am.* After eating she stopped at the liquor store and bought two bottles of vodka and a case of Coke. She put one bottle in her trunk. She could stay at work and eat.

She went back to the motel. It was dark, and no one was around, so she quickly dug up the bottle and took four out and reburied it. She poured herself a vodka on the rocks. She was bored. She couldn't get the thought of doing cocaine out of her mind. She was pretty sure Dr. Crusher wouldn't be in his office, but she decided to call. She dialed the number and got his answering service. She left her name number and said it was an emergency. She decided to wait a little while to see if he would call back before taking the pills. She lay on the bed, sipping her vodka. To her surprise, in about a half an hour, her phone rang. It was the doctor.

She sang out, "Doctor, Doctor, I think I'm going to crash. Can you help me?"

The doctor answered back, "I'm all alone and I'm horny. Can you help me?"

Sandy told him, "I can help you any way you want for a couple of those big lines of white powder."

He gave her his address and said, "Wear something sexy."

She was glad that she had her black leather costume cleaned. She put it on with her knee-high boots and brought along her cat o' nine tails. She thought he might just get a big kick out of being wiped. She put on her long black gloves and packed a little bag that had jeans and a blouse in it. It would be really late when she would be driving home, and just in case she got stopped by the cops, it would be hard to explain her costume. It wasn't Halloween. She was a little paranoid with her court date coming up so soon.

Dr. Crusher told her he would leave the door unlocked, just to come in, and then lock the door behind her. When she entered the house, he had left a paper trail of notes, saying to meet him in the garage. She couldn't imagine why, but at that point, she would have met him on the roof. She opened the door and said, "Are you in here?"

"Yes, and there are two big lines on the top of the dryer just waiting for you."

She walked to the dryer, and there they were along with his little gold straw. She wasted no time snorting both of them. "I can hear you, but I don't know where you are. I need a little vodka."

He said, "If you must, there's a bottle in the freezer."

She went back inside, got the bottle, then went back to the garage. "What are we doing in here?"

He said, "Just have a couple of shots and get relaxed. Then I'll tell you."

She took a couple of big gulps. "Are you playing hide and seek with me?"

"Kind of." He had an antique Volkswagen Beetle parked in the middle of the huge garage. "Come around to the other side. I really like your costume." He was lying naked on the floor with a ski between his legs lined up with one of the tires. Sandy couldn't understand what the hell he was doing. "You see that line coming down from the ceiling that has a weight on the end?"

She looked up. "Yes."

He told her that he wanted her to get in the car and pull forward until the weight hit the hood of the car then stop. "It is a stick shift. Have you ever driven one?"

"That's what I drive."

"When you get to that point, take your foot off the gas and push the clutch in. The car will roll back."

She said, "What! Are you crazy?"

"I have done this before. I have the logistics worked out perfectly. Don't ask any more questions if you want to do a couple more lines. I've left a little baggie in the car. So get in and do what I've ask."

She was high and a little drunk, but if this was what he wanted, then that's what she would do to get a couple of more lines. She got in the car and started it. She yelled out the window, "Are you sure?"

"Yes, just do it."

She put the bug in first gear and stepped on the gas. The weight hit the hood. She put it in neutral and let it roll back. She got out and ran around to where he was. "Are you okay?"

"Yes, that was perfect." He held out his hand for her to help him up. Sandy got the baggie out the car. "Is this for me to take home?"

"Yes, I have more. Have another drink. I'll be back in a minute." Sandy took the bottle and sat down in the living room. Dr. Crusher came out wearing a pair of leather pants with the butt cheeks cut out.

"How cute we match." Sandy asked him, "I don't understand, what do you get out of that?"

"It's all about the pressure and the intensity. Pain can be very pleasurable if you're in the right mind-set."

She took another drink and then passed the bottle to him. "How did you ever get started on this path to pain to pleasure?"

"It started when I was a boy. My sister and I would play cops and robbers. I would always be the robber. She, the cop. When she caught me, she would hold me down and slap my face. It didn't hurt. It felt good and I would tell her harder. It just progressed from there. I would have her stand on my hands. One day, I had her stand on my chest I couldn't breathe. But it gave me a feeling of euphoria and I came. That was the first time I ever had an ejaculation."

Sandy told him about her first sexual experience and how she had a climax experienced that same feeling. They finished the bottle of vodka and snorted a couple more lines. He told Sandy to lie on the floor with her arms over her head with her hand stretched out. She wasn't sure that she really wanted to do that, but he assured her he would stop if she told him to. He stood on one hand and then the other. She cried out stop. He told her just to relax and take in the feeling of being helpless. She could relate to that feeling of hopelessness. That's the feeling she had most of her life. As she let her brain drift back into the past of all the lost she had felt, the pain went away. Dr. Crusher stepped back off her hands.

"Can you understand how pain can turn to pleasure?"

"I think I can. It's late. I have to go." She changed into her jeans and blouse. She thanked him for the cocaine.

"I am still curious about this pain-to-pleasure thing. Maybe we can get together some other time and explore it."

She drove home being a little paranoid about having the cocaine in the car with her. She felt absolutely joyful when she pulled into the motel's parking lot. She still felt confused about pain to pleasure. She took a bath and brushed her teeth. She took two of the pills and another glass of vodka and fell asleep.

12

When she woke up, she had a little bit of a hangover. She was tempted to do a line. She decided just to take a bath and get dressed. The only other white blouse she owned was peasant style. Her black pants didn't fit her like a glove, but they still looked good. She got to work at 7:45 a.m. She wanted to make sure that she had her assigned area before Wayne came in. Her stations were full, and there wasn't an empty seat. When Wayne got there, she went over to him.

"There is no empty seat in my area." She hoped he wasn't I in a hurry. "Could you wait a few minutes until a table is available?"

"I'd wait an hour if that meant being able to talk to you."

He only had to wait about fifteen minutes. She had the busboy clean the table right away. She ushered him to have a seat. She brought him a menu. He smiled up at her. "I haven't had this feeling in a very long time. I can't keep you off my mind." She brought him a cup of coffee.

"I see you're wearing a wedding band."

He looked down at his hand. "Yes, I am married. But I'm not in love. Once our children were grown, I realized that was the glue that held our marriage together. I love my wife because she is the mother of our children. I'm not in love with her anymore."

Sandy had to stop him. She had other tables she needed to wait on. When she brought Wayne his breakfast, she said, "If you want to continue this conversation, I get off at four."

Wayne took her hand and said, "I'll meet you in the parking lot."

The day seemed to drag and Sandy couldn't get Wayne off her mine. She still didn't want to start anything until she had her court date behind her. She wanted to explain to Wayne her circumstances. There was no doubt that she felt an attraction to him, but he was married. She knew from the past that married men rarely ever left their wives.

When her shift was over, she hurried to the parking lot. Wayne wasn't there. She got the bottle of vodka out of her trunk and took a couple of big sips and put it back. Wayne drove up just a couple of minutes after that. She walked over to his truck, and he opened the door. She got in.

Sandy asked, "What are we doing? You are married and you don't even really know me."

Wayne took her hand. "I don't know what I am doing. All I know I wanted to see you. Not only at work but after." He leaned toward her and kissed her. She still didn't know what she was doing, but it felt good and she kissed him back.

As Sandy pulled away, she looked at him. "My life is complicated, and I'm not really sure about my future."

Wayne grabbed her and kissed her again. "I am not sure about my future either, but I do know I want you in it."

Sandy leaned back. "You just met me. You don't know anything about me. You've only known me for the last two days. We don't know what's been in our past that might affect our future."

Wayne had a hard time keeping his hands off her. "I don't care what's in your past. You're not wearing a wedding ring. I take it you're not married."

Sandy picked up his hand. "You are wearing a wedding band and that means you are committed to someone else. How do you think you or I could start a future with you still being married? These feelings could just be an escape from your reality."

Wayne looked deeply into her eyes. "Do you believe in love at first sight? That everything happens for a reason? I know it was fate that morning I came into the restaurant and you waited on my table. I felt it the first moment I saw you. That has never happened to me before. I have met a lot of women, some being a little friendlier than they should have. Not once did I have an attraction to them. So how do you explain that when I saw you I felt like my whole life had changed?"

Sandy wanted to believe him. It just seemed too good to be true. She wanted them to go someplace and have a couple of drinks and talk things over. Wayne told her that he would love to, but he had a prior engagement that had to do with his business. He couldn't miss it. Sandy got out of the truck, feeling a little disappointed. She waved by as he drove away.

After he drove away, she remembered that she had not told him she wouldn't be at work tomorrow. Maybe that would be a good thing.

Even if it would only be for one day, that would give both of them a little space to think things over. She had known so many men that had either let her down or left or died that she was apprehensive about thinking that there could ever be a happy ending.

As she was driving home, she went over the words he said in her mind. Was there love at first sight? She could honestly say that she didn't feel that about Wayne the first time she saw him. She felt a physical attraction, but being as sexual as she was, she couldn't even say that she did not love Mr. X at first sight. She really didn't know how much she had loved him until he was gone. Hope and she had started off as friends. It was all the different circumstances that she and Hope had experienced that brought them together, and their feelings had turned to love. Tears ran down her cheeks. Thinking of them, she was filled with great sorrow. It was impossible for her to believe that she had lost both of the people that she had loved so close together. It made her hesitate about falling in love again. She didn't think she could bear that pain again and still survive.

As she drove home, she couldn't help but think about court. She hoped her lawyer and Jean were right She would only get probation. She needed to get a good night's rest so she would look fresh in the morning. She had one conservative dress that she used to wear to church. Pulling her hair up into a ponytail gave her a more-youthful look. She wanted the judge to see her as a young woman that just made a mistake. She rehearsed what she would say to the judge if she were asked, "I'm so sorry. I have already learned my lesson. I plan to work hard and get my life straightened out. I promise that you will never see me in court again."

She arrived at court two hours before her hearing. She looked around to see if she could find her lawyer Mr. Hargreaves. To her surprise, Jean was there. She came walking toward her and asked, "Are you looking for Mr. Hargreaves."

"Yes, have you seen him?"

"No, but he's to meet with me this morning also." Sandy told Jean that he had said she would probably only get probation.

"I wish that I would only get probation, but this is the third time I have been arrested for solicitation. I might just have to do a little time in the pokey." Jean said to Sandy, "You know, if you get probation for drugs, you will be drug tested."

Sandy had a very worried look on her face. Jean said, "Don't tell me you're still doing drugs." Sandy just nodded yes. "They could ask for a urine sample today."

Sandy asked Jean, "Do you do drugs?"

"No."

"If I can find a little container, would you pee in it for me?"

"Yes, but we will have to hurry. Mr. Hargreaves should be here any second." Sandy went to the vending machine and got a bottle of water, and she and Jean went to the bathroom. She emptied the water out and ran the bottle under hot water. They also went by temperature. Jean peed into the bottle.

"I hope this works out for you, kid. If you test dirty while you're on probation, you will go to jail."

Sandy felt sick to her stomach. The thought of being in jail was overwhelming. The thought of not being able to do any drugs for however long she was on probation made her feel even sicker.

Sandy had a large purse that she put the bottle in. When they came out of the bathroom, Mr. Hargreaves was looking for them. He pulled Sandy aside. "We didn't get too lucky. The judge is a real stickler. I'm still hoping you only get probation, but he might add some hours of community service to your sentence. We'll just have to hope for the best." Then he walked over to Jean. Sandy could hear what he was saying. "This is your third time. This judge is a real hard nose. I am pretty sure you are going to get jail time."

The bailiff came to the door and announced, "Court is now in session."

Sandy and Jane followed Mr. Hargreaves and took a seat.

Right before the judge came in, the bailiff said, "All stand," and then once the judge was seated, they all sat down. They called case after case. The longer that they didn't call her number, the more worried she got. Jean's number was called, case 483. It didn't make much sense to her that they didn't call the cases in order. Mr. Hargreaves and Jean stood up.

"I see, Ms. Johnson, that you are quite familiar with the court system. I believe this is your third time being arrested for solicitation. You have pled guilty. Do you have anything to say for yourself?"

"Yes, Your Honor. I don't have any other skills. No one will hire me because I don't have any education. I have to do what I know I do best. I wish I lived a different lifestyle. In a perfect world, women wouldn't be prosecuted for what gentlemen need. I believe I do society a perfectly normal convenience. Just think of how many more divorces there would be if men didn't have women like me to turn to."

The judge banged his gavel. "It is still against the law, Ms. Johnson. You are sentenced to sixty days in the county jail. Next."

Several more cases were called, and then Sandy's number came up. She and Mr. Hargreaves stood up.

"I see you have pled guilty."

"Yes, Your Honor."

"This is the first time you've been in court. Do you have anything to say before I pass sentencing?"

She gave her little rehearsed answer. "I'm going to send one of our female bailiffs with you to get a urine sample. If it tests negative, I will be inclined to give you probation. If it tests dirty, I think thirty days in the county jail will give you time to decide what you want to do with the rest of your life."

She and the bailiff went to a restroom. The bailiff said, "I have to watch you."

"Really, I can't pee in a bottle with you watching me. I have a shy bladder. What do you think I should do? This is my first time in court. I didn't know the judge would ask for a urine sample."

The bailiff said, "Against my better judgment, I will wait outside."

Sandy breathed a sigh of relief. She got the bottle out of her purse and poured the urine into the sample bottle that the bailiff had given her. She squeezed all the air out of the bottle to compress it. She put it in the back of the toilet She came out and the bailiff said, "I have to check the restroom to make sure that you urinated into the container." She went into the restroom and dug through the garbage and then told Sandy to empty her purse. When all that was done, the bailiff felt confident that the sample was Sandy's.

13

When they came back into the courtroom, Sandy sat down beside Mr. Hargreaves. When the judge got finished with the case and the sentencing, he called 321, her number. She and Mr. Hargreaves stood up.

"I'm glad to see that you tested negative. I'm giving you six months' probation and two hundred hours of community service. Mr. Hargreaves will give you a list of businesses that participate in this program. You are to see your probation officer once a month, and you will be drug tested." He banged his gavel and said, "Next."

They walked outside. "Do you have the list of programs that I can participate in?"

"Yes, I keep a copy of them in my briefcase." He took the list out and handed it to her. The list included helping out at a nursing home, working behind a cafeteria line at a local hospital, helping the city pick up trash along the highways, or helping out at the local animal shelter. Out of all the choices, she thought helping out at the animal shelter would be the thing that she would enjoy the most.

"You will have to do eight hours every week, and you'll still have eight hours to make up."

"I work from eight in the morning until four in the afternoon. How late is the shelter open?"

"I believe until six o'clock. Then on my day off, I will work eight hours and, some weeks, ten."

He looked at her. "It is very important that you complete your community service before we go back to court. You must test clean on your drug tests. I know this judge, and if you failed to do either of these things, he will give you thirty days in the county jail. Are we perfectly clear?"

"Yes, sir." She shook his hand. "I appreciate all that you've done for me. I won't let you down."

As Sandy drove home, she wondered how long it would take for all the drugs to get out of her system. She could find that information on the internet. She knew there were certain herbs you could take that would help clean your system quicker. The thought of spending thirty days in the county jail sent a shiver up her spine. He said drugs did not include alcohol. She would call Mr. Hargreaves later to find out. She wasn't really sure how she could not at least drink for six months and keep her sanity.

Wayne came to her mind. If she couldn't drink, she would be forced to tell him about court and its demands. She tried to convince herself that wouldn't matter to him. This would be a good thing. She knew it would be better for her to quit drinking and taking drugs. She had done them for so long she was worried about how her body would react not having a drink in eight to ten hours. Her hands would start shaking and her stomach hurting. Just thinking about it made her want a drink and a couple of her little helpers and a big line of cocaine. This was going to be a lot tougher than she ever imagined.

Her phone rang. She let it go to voice mail. It was the detective that was investigating Hope's death. He wanted her to come down to the station. He had more questions. Fear surrounded her like a cage. Now she would have to go and meet him without being able to take anything to calm her nerves. She had to be at work by eight and wouldn't get off until four. She had already taken today off, and there wasn't any way she could take off tomorrow. She would simply have to tell him that she wouldn't be able to meet with him until after five tomorrow.

When she reached the motel, she decided she might as well call the detective and get it over with. When he answered the phone, she said, "This is Sandy Nash. You wanted to speak to me."

The voice on the other end of the line said, "Yes, I would like you to come back down to the station."

Sandy told him, "I work from eight to four tomorrow."

He told her that she could come down now. She froze. She wasn't prepared to be questioned. He insisted that she come down to the sheriff's office as soon as possible. "I will be expecting you within the hour." She would normally have a couple of stiff drinks. Now she would have to go cold turkey.

Driving to the station, she put her air conditioner on full blast. She didn't want to be all sweaty when she got there. Pulling into the parking lot, fear set in. She told herself over and over again to be calm.

"Your answers will be 'I don't know anything, I didn't see anything, I didn't hear anything. Other than that, I have already told you.'"

Detective Jones was waiting for her. He took her back to the same little room that he had questioned her in before. Sandy sat down and he sat across from her. Her forehead was already starting to sweat.

The detective told her, "Hope's autopsy had come back. She died of a heart attack that was brought on by cocaine. The other thing that the autopsy revealed were multiple fractures of her ribs, right arm in two places, her wrist, and one to her skull. You said she had a jealous boyfriend and that she told you he was violent. Did you ever see him strike her?"

She knew the police would ask leading questions, hoping you would slip up and not give the same answer you had given before.

"No, sir, I already told you that I never met him. She shared a few stories about him beating her."

Jones told her that he had been unable to locate her boyfriend. "It seems as if you were telling the truth about her not being able to take anyone home. None of the other girls at the shop nor the owner, David, knew anything about him. We did locate her mother in Nebraska. Her family are Mormons. Her mother told me that Hope had been faithful to their beliefs until she met a man. After that, everything changed. They never met him, and one day, Hope disappeared, leaving a note behind— sorry she loved them, but she loved her boyfriend more. They never heard from her again. She is coming to claim the body and take her back home so she can have a proper funeral. I heard you had your court date today?"

"Yes, sir."

"What happened?"

"I got six months' probation, two hundred hours of community service. I have to check in with my probation officer once a month and be drug tested. Can I ask you something? Does that mean no alcohol either?"

He looked up with raised eyebrows. "Alcohol is not an illegal drug. You weren't arrested for anything that was related to alcohol. It would probably be a good thing for you not to drink. Call your probation officer and ask them."

"Why am I here?"

He replied, "So far, we have been unable to find an address where Hope was living. The address that she gave at work was an abandoned building that had been condemned. I just wanted to make sure that there wasn't anything else you could tell us about her that might help us find her boyfriend. The car that she was driving was impounded. It had a stolen tag and had never been registered. Did you ever see what kind of vehicle her boyfriend drove?"

"No, I'm sorry I can't help you." Sandy knew the detective was trying to trip her up again with his questions. "I have already told you that I never met him and never saw his car. If that's all, I really need to go."

As she walked outside, she breathed a sigh of relief. She hoped that would be the last time she would have to talk to him. Now she was thinking about what the detective said. Alcohol wasn't an illegal drug. She wanted to stop and buy a bottle of vodka. Her hands were shaking, and she felt a little sick to her stomach. That was her body telling her it needed a drink. When she got back to the motel, she took the papers that Mr. Hargreaves had given her to find the number for her probation officer. She called the number and asked to speak to Loretta Fisher who was her assigned probation officer. They connected her to her office.

"Mrs. Fisher—how may I help you?"

"I'm Sandy Nash. I've been assigned to you."

"Yes, I received your papers."

"I wanted to know if I could drink alcohol. I know I am being tested for illegal and prescription drugs."

"Your probation state drugs, not alcohol. I must tell you if you are arrested again, you will not only be breaking your probation, but the new charges would be added on to your sentence. I would advise you not to drink." Sandy thanked Mrs. Fisher and ask what the date was that she need to see her.

"The first of every month."

"I work from eight to four. Can I come in before or after work?"

"My office is open from seven in the morning until six at night." Sandy thanked her again and hung up.

She went straight to her car and drove to the liquor store. She bought two bottles of vodka. As soon as she got back to the motel, she poured herself a drink. She drank it quickly and poured another. In a short while, her hands stopped shaking and the pain in her stomach went away. She hadn't eaten anything all day. She decided before she had another drink she had better go and get something to eat. There was a fast-food restaurant called Good and Plenty with a drive-through about a mile from her motel. It specialized in barbecue. That wasn't her first choice, but it would do. She got a barbecue pork sandwich with coleslaw and a large soda. She waited until she got back to the motel to eat. When she was finished, she poured herself another drink. She lay down on the bed and thought about seeing Wayne tomorrow. After she finished her drink, she took off all her clothes. Then she crawled back into bed. Wayne was still on her mind. She fantasized about how good of a lover he would be. She hadn't had any real sex with a man since Mr. X died. She fell asleep imagining that Wayne was lying beside her. In her dream, he was a dashing prince that had rescued her from all the evil in the world. When he gazed into her eyes, she was filled with joy. He told her that he had never loved anyone so deeply as he loved her. If she would trust him, they would have the most magnificent life together. When she woke the next morning, the dream had been so vivid she had a hard time believing that it had been just a dream.

She got up a little early, took a bath, and curled her hair She wanted to look her very best when she saw Wayne. When she arrived at work, Mary noticed right away that she had a big smile on her face.

"Everything must have gone well yesterday? You got your mother's affairs in order?"

"Yes, I think everything is going to work out."

She went to the area that she had been assigned, and in between waiting on customers, she kept looking at the door. It was eight thirty, and Wayne had not come in. It was hard for her to keep her mind on work. She must have looked at the door twenty times. When her shift was over, she couldn't understand why he had not come in for breakfast. Then she remembered that she hadn't told him that she wouldn't be at work yesterday. She wanted to ask one of the other servers if he had been in yesterday. She decided not to ask because he was married, and she didn't want to start any gossip about them. She thought about calling his work cell phone. She decided not to call and just wait and see if he would come for breakfast tomorrow. She felt so anxious that she couldn't wait to get home and have a couple of drinks. Maybe even a couple more. She didn't want to think about Wayne. She knew herself that her imagination would run wild, but she couldn't help it. Maybe he had been a jerk just like most of the men she knew. Or he was a fabulous liar and that's the way he got his kicks. He was sick or got in a car accident or had just simply changed his mind about her. She tried to put those thoughts aside. After six vodkas, she could hardly think at all. She fell asleep crying.

At work the next day, Wayne never came in. On her break, she took his card out of her purse and tore it into pieces. She didn't want to be tempted to call him. For the rest of the week, she couldn't help but glance at the door, hoping he would walk through it. That didn't happen, nor did it the next week. She had settled into a rut, going to work, grabbing a bite to eat on the way home, and drinking until she fell asleep. She was so depressed that she didn't even go to the dog shelter the week before. Now she was eight hours behind. Monday she had to go. There wouldn't be any way for her to make up for sixteen hours. She loved animals and hoped working with them would cheer her up.

On Monday, she realized summer was almost over. There was a chill in the air. She drove to the shelter. It was much bigger than she had pictured. She asked to speak to the person in charge.

"I am. How can I help you?"

"I'm Sandy Nash. I'm here to do my community service."

"I am Mr. Rosenblum. Come into my office. We have some paperwork regarding the program." After they had finished, he took her back to the kennels. He introduced her to Matt. "He will show you what to do."

Matt was tall over six feet and had a chiseled face that was so handsome Sandy couldn't help but stare. He motioned for her to come with him. They walked back to the cages where the dogs were kept in.

"I'll take the dogs out of their cages one by one, and you need to take the hose and wash them." He took the first dog out. It was a cute little wiener dog.

Sandy squatted down and asked, "Is it okay if I pet him?"

"Yes, but you can't take the time to pat each dog or we'll never get our work done today."

One by one, she washed the cages. She couldn't believe how many unwanted animals there were. She wished she had a place where she could at least take a couple of them. The day went by quickly and Matt and she made a little small talk. He never asked her what she had done to get community service. When her eight hours were up, she told him that she needed to make up for the day that she missed, so I could stay a little longer?

"My shift is over. You will have to go back in and talk to Mr. Rosenblum."

They walked back to the front together. "I have enjoyed working with you today."

Sandy smiled at him. "I have enjoyed today. It didn't seem like a punishment."

As he left the building, he said, "See you next week."

She knocked on Mr. Rosenblum's door. "Come in."

"I was wondering if I could stayed a little longer to help make up for the eight hours I missed."

"You can stay until six. That's when we close."

"If I can do this every time, I will complete my hours before I have to go back to court."

"We can always use all the help we can get. It's time to start feeding the dogs. Joe Lee will help you." They walked back to the kennels and he introduced her to Joe Lee. "Sandy will be helping you." They went inside a storage room where they kept the dog food.

"You can hand me the dishes and I'll fill them. Each dish has the cage number on it. After filling ten, we will take them to the cages and keep repeating this until they're all fed. After they have finished eating, we collect the dishes and wash and dry them." Sandy enjoyed getting to take the time to give each of them a little pet. Joe Lee shared with her that she was doing community hours also. Sandy told her that she had gotten two hundred hours for having contraband.

"I got three hundred hours plus losing my license for drunk driving."

"How do you get back and forth from where you live to the shelter?"

"A friend of mine drops me off and Mr. Rosenblum takes me home. He is a very nice man, nonjudgmental."

14

When the shelter closed, the three of them walked out together. Sandy told Mr. Rosenblum how much she had enjoyed the day.

She couldn't wait to get home. It had been ten hours without a drink and she was starting to feel the effects. She wasn't hungry, so she didn't stop to buy anything. When she reached the motel, she hurried inside and poured herself a drink. She kicked off her shoes and lay down on the bed. She thought about how handsome Matt was, and he wasn't wearing a wedding band. She thought about how many men had been in her life, and in one way or another, they had all let her down. Starting with her father. He died just at a point in her life that she needed him most. He left her with the responsibility and the decision to institutionalized her mother permanently unless a miracle happened. She didn't believe in miracles. She really wasn't sure why she felt the sudden urge to see her. That wouldn't be possible until she had completed her obligations to the court. She felt all confused inside. Why didn't any of her relationships work out? It couldn't have been the fault of all the men in her lives. That left only one person to blame—herself.

She had an eerie feeling sometimes that she wasn't making the decisions in her life herself. On occasion, her thoughts were so scrambled as if there were two of her playing tug-of-war. These strange occurrences made her feel as if she were going mad like her mother.

She would have to go and see her probation officer after work tomorrow. She had been taking the herbs that were supposed to help clear the drugs out of her system. Tomorrow would be showtime. It made her very nervous to think she might fail. She had a couple more drinks and fell asleep. It was a restless sleep. She kept seeing herself in a stripe uniform. She kept wanting to explain to someone that it wasn't her fault. All the bad things that she had done was her reflection in the mirror, not her.

At work the next day, they were exceptionally busy. The tables that had her men that came in almost every day were very generous. She made more tips that one day than she had in the previous two days. Maybe it was the worried and desperate look she had on her face. She kept having flashbacks of her dream. Now it was time to go to her appointment and see if she would test negative. She always hated stripes. (Person____)

When she got to the parking lot, she wished she had gone home and had a drink. Her nerves were shot. She went inside. There wasn't anybody waiting. Mrs. Fisher took her right back to her office. She handed her a sampling cup. She had to leave her purse outside the bathroom. She took the cup. When she came out, she handed it to Mrs. Fisher. She was saying a little prayer for herself and keeping her fingers crossed.

"Negative, you have tested negative. The first month is always the hardest. It should get easier as time goes on. You won't think about taking drugs as often."

Sandy wondered if Mrs. Fisher had ever had an addiction to anything. If she had, she would know that it never got easier. Possible, yes, but not easier.

At work the next day, she thought she saw Wayne's truck drive by. She discounted it as wishful thinking. The restaurant had steadily become busier. It was October and the snowbirds were coming back. There were a lot of new faces, most of them older. They weren't big tippers. She had to work harder to get them in and out. The faster she could turn the tables around, the more money. She was finding it hard to keep that pace up day after day. It made it difficult for her to give the attention to her regulars. Somehow, she made time to give them a smile or pat them on the back and tell them she was so happy to see them among all the strangers. Apparently, that made them feel good. On occasion, they would even leave a bigger tip.

The weeks flew by, and Mondays seem to even come quicker. Matt and she and Joe Lee had become friends. Joe Lee had started coming in during the day when she could. She needed to complete her hours. In the beginning, she had missed quite a few days, and now that her court date was coming up, she was trying desperately to make them up. She found out that Matt was also doing community service. He had gotten in a fight and had put the other man in the hospital. He was charged with assault and battery and had spent three years in prison. They let him out on good behavior early, but he was given six hundred hours of community service. He was also having to take anger management classes. Sandy thought that they had been doing him a lot of good. He was soft-spoken, and she never once saw him lose his temper. On occasion, the three of them would go out after the shelter closed to get a bite to eat. Sandy had the feeling that she had some real friends. She had not had that since Hope died. Terry and she had been good friends, but she hadn't seen her since she left the shop. When she got time, maybe she would give her a call. They hadn't been as close once she got married.

As the weeks and months went by, Matt and Sandy had gone out a few times alone. They didn't tell Joe Lee. They didn't want to hurt her feelings. She was such a sweet girl. They both knew they had feelings for each other.

Because of their circumstances, they had limit their feelings to just kissing. They talked about when they were finished with all their obligations to the court, maybe they could become more involved. For the time being, they had to be careful not to draw attention to their friendship outside the shelter. It was illegal. If you were on probation, you could not be involved with another felon. Sandy never drank around Matt or Joe Lee. Sandy found it easier than she thought it would be not to drink until she got home.

It was mid-November and Thanksgiving was coming up. The restaurant had already taken reservations, and they were almost completely booked. Matt and Joe Lee had no family in the area. Sandy bought them a gift certificate so they could come and eat at the restaurant. Employees got a 15 percent discount. With them there, even though she would be serving, she felt as if she had a family. All three of them felt, in one way or another, that they were family. Sandy had let the walls come down and allowed herself to be vulnerable. It scared her but that was the only way she could let someone in and maybe fall in love. That's the thing she wanted the most.

Joe Lee never talked about having a boyfriend. She was 5"1' and a little on the chubby side. She had a cute little face with a turned-up nose. Her hair was cut short in a pixie, and she never wore makeup. One evening, after working at the shelter, Sandy asked her if she would like to come back to the motel.

"I'd like that a lot."

When they left the shelter, she stopped and got them Chinese for dinner. When they reached the motel, Sandy took out her bottle of vodka and poured herself a drink. "I hope this doesn't bother you. I like to have a couple of drinks before I eat. My probation is only for drugs not alcohol."

"They test me for everything under the sun. I don't dare even take an aspirin."

After they ate, Sandy mentioned, "I noticed you never wear makeup. I was a hairstylist and did a lot of wedding parties including their makeup. I'd love to show you how I could enhance your eyes and cheekbones."

Joe Lee looked down. "I'm not trying to attract a man."

"What does that mean?"

"Can't you guess? I'm gay."

For a moment, Sandy didn't know what to say. "I've had a lot of gay friends being in the hair business."

Joe Lee stood up. "For some reason, I just thought you knew."

"Does Matt know?"

"If you're asking me did I ever tell him, no. If he has thought it, he never mentioned it to me or let on. He's my first real male friend. I always shied away from men before. Afraid of getting beat up or something. You know how some males can be very prejudiced, especially the macho ones."

Sandy took her hand and gave it a little pat. "I love you just the way you are. For who you are, not what you are."

Joe Lee took her hand from Sandy's and stepped back. "You wouldn't be interested, would you?"

"I think you're wonderful and I really like you. I love you as if you were family. We have such a good relationship. Why mess it up?"

Joe Lee hugged her. "We're still friends, right?"

"Of course this doesn't change anything. Let's not talk about it in front of Matt. We all have such a good time together. I don't want anything to change. I don't think it would, but you never know. It's getting late, and I have to work tomorrow. I better drive you home."

On the way back home, Sandy kept thinking about Joe Lee being gay. Usually, she would pick up on a thing like that. She was very fond of Joe Lee, but she wasn't her type. She startled herself, saying out loud, "I guess I'm bisexual. I never thought about it before."

Most of her sexual experiences had been with men, but there was that redhead and Hope. I think most people put in the right circumstances may have a bisexual experience. Sex is sex. Does it really make that much difference? She remembered when same-sex couples could legally get married. All the protesters and God-fearing people saying it was an abomination. She didn't really care what two adults chose to do. It wasn't hers or anybody else's business. Some people like to make everything their business. That's what they live for stirring up trouble, making other people miserable. She had met a few people like that They were the ones that should be protested against for just being alive. A few customers and one in particular. She would always talk about going to church every Sunday, singing in the choir, and holding Bible meeting at her house. In the next breath, she'd be telling you that she knew black people by the use of the N word were the cause of most of the problems in this country. Sandy always wanted to ask her what color was their God, but she had to bite her tongue.

"If I had known I was going to lose my job, there would have been a few people that I would have loved to have shared my opinion. I guess, in the long run, it was better that I didn't know."

15

Thanksgiving Day had arrived. Sandy went into work a little early to help with preparations. The restaurant had a policy that any of the employees or ex-employees that wanted to celebrate Thanksgiving at the restaurant after it closed were welcome. On occasion, some of them brought family members. It had been this way for the past five years. The owners, Lucy and James Crookes, didn't have any family in the area. So this was not only for the employees but for them. Everybody could get caught up on the gossip and special events that had happened. There were a lot of laughing but also a few tears.

She had told Joe Lee and Matt to be at the restaurant at eleven forty-five. She had a nice corner booth waiting for them. Neither of them cooked. They lived off snacks, sandwiches, and frozen dinners. She could tell just by looking at them that they were really excited to have a real Thanksgiving. The restaurant was full. There wasn't one empty chair.

"We have two choices, ham or turkey."

They both said turkey. "It wouldn't seem like Thanksgiving if we didn't have turkey."

She quickly went and found Mary. "My two closest friends don't have anybody to celebrate Thanksgiving with. Would it be okay if I had them come to the employee's dinner?"

"I think we can squeeze two more in."

She hurried back to Matt and Joe Lee's table. "I have really good news for you. I asked my floor manager if I could invite you to the employee's dinner after the restaurant closes. You can have ham tonight. That way, you get to try both of them."

Joe Lee took one of Sandy's hands. "This is the best Thanksgiving I have ever had. None of the people in my family get along, so we really didn't celebrate too many of the holidays. My mother said it was a lot to do over nothing, and what did she have to be grateful for, married to a time bomb and living in a broke-down trailer?"

The day flew by. It was six o'clock and the last customer had left. All the servers were anxious to count their tips. The mood had been good in the restaurant all day. The servers were happy and cheery and tried their very best to give their customers really good service. Apparently, they had all made a. hundred or better. Now it was time to get everything cleaned up so they could celebrate with their friends and employers. Lucy and James, the owners, had been the best. If you needed a day off or even a week you didn't have to worry about losing your job. Everything was clean and ready. They served it buffet style, so no one had to wait on anyone else. The families of cooks Roman, Norman, and Kevin and the prep chef Louise had started to arrive. Sandy kept looking for Matt and Joe Lee. There must have been at least seventy-five people there. She finally saw them at the back of the line. Sandy was anxious to meet some of her coworkers' friends and family. Norman talked a lot about his beautiful girlfriend and her little daughter. No one ever said anything about Roman and Kevin being a couple. Louise was middle-aged and divorced. She was very quiet and really didn't share any of her intimate details of her life.

When all had taken a seat, James and Lucy stood up. "I want to thank each and every one of you for being so loyal. I cannot imagine having a better group of people working for me. Let the celebration begin."

The bar had a variety of red and white wines, iced tea, coffee, and sodas. One by one, the tables got up and got their beverage. Then they went to the buffets and served themselves. When Matt was walking back to his table, he saw a familiar face. He was stunned. He stopped dead in his tracks. He couldn't believe what his eyes were seeing.

The girlfriend of Norman, one of the cooks, had been the reason Matt was sent to prison. Looking at her daughter, he could see she had the same green color of his eyes.

His memories took him back to the night he was arrested. Sarah and he had been walking on Pier 60. She had on string bikini with a see-through cover-up. Two drunks walked by, and one of them said, "How much for a piece of that?" Matt grabbed him and wanted him to apologize.

The drunk man said, "You don't dress like that unless you want to give a little pussy away."

Matt saw red. He lost all control. He grabbed the man and pushed him to the pavement and started hitting him over and over again. The man was so drunk he really couldn't defend himself. The next thing Matt knew, he was being handcuffed and taken to jail. Once he got there and they had finished booking him, he gave Sarah a call.

"Can you come and bail me out?"

"I don't have any extra money. You know I'm struggling."

She didn't bail him out. It was two months before his court date came up. She never went to see him. His heart was broken. She had been the love of his life. Apparently, her feelings were not the same. He was convicted on assault and battery charges and given four and a half years and three years of probation and six hundred hours of community service.

He walked over to Sarah. She had not noticed him. Her eyes flew open wide and her face went pale.

"Matt, what are you doing here?"

"I was invited by a friend. What are you doing here?"

"I lived with one of the cooks, Norman."

"Is that your daughter?"

"Yes!"

"How old is she?"

"Almost five."

"She has my eyes. Is she my daughter?"

"Yes, I didn't want to tell you. You were going to prison. The night you were arrested, I wasn't sure that I was pregnant. I knew my period was late. The next day, I took one of those home pregnancy test. It was positive. Being pregnant, I knew my whole life would change. You had a bad temper, and I didn't want to expose my child to that."

"You mean *our* child."

"Norman came into my life when I really needed somebody. Even though he knew he wasn't the father, he has been the only father that she has known. He loves her and me. We are in a really good spot."

"Can I at least know my daughter's name?"

"Lana Marie. I named her after my mother and grandmother. She has my last name, Williams. I had to go on welfare. I told the welfare workers that I had a one-night stand and didn't know who the father was. I didn't want to make it any worse for you. They go after deadbeat fathers that don't pay child support and take away their driver's license. I thought when you did get out of prison, you certainly didn't need any more complications. I did love you. That's why I lied about not knowing who the father was. Norman thinks the same thing. He never held it against me getting pregnant by somebody he thought I didn't even know. He told me it was better that way. There wouldn't be any one coming to interfere with our lives. I hope you understand, Matt, that I was doing the best I could for myself, my child, and you. I really have to go back to my table. I don't want Norman to ask me too many questions about you. If he does, I am simply going to say that we were friends a long time ago."

Sandy and Joe Lee were wondering why Matt had been talking to Norman's girlfriend. When he came back to the table, they asked him.

"She was a friend of mine a long time ago. I had not seen her in years. We just wanted to get caught up on what has happened since the last time we saw each other."

Sandy couldn't help but notice that the curly-headed strawberry blond little girl had Matt's green eyes. Matt excused himself, saying, "All that rich food in one day made my stomach hurt. I'm just not used to it. I'm going home."

As Matt left the table, Joe Lee looked at Sandy. "Something doesn't make sense."

Sandy told her, "Sometimes, it's better not to ask questions. We all have skeletons in our closet that need to remain there. Those things that we want to keep private, sometimes if people know that would be all that they would take into consideration. That doesn't always define us as a person. I believe the day I meet someone that person has a clean slate. It is not my business to dig up their past."

After all the celebrating and eating was done, Joe Lee help clean up. Sandy offered to give her a ride home.

"That would be great. I hate having to rely upon my friend Sam. I know he really doesn't mind, but it will be nice when I can be a little more independent. He is my roommate. We went to high school together. I think we were the only gay people in the whole school. Some bigmouth found out. I don't know how, but it spread all around the school. After that, we might as well had the plague. We bonded over that experience and have been best friends since. He is sweet and kind and doesn't have a mean bone in his body. That's the kind of woman I'm looking for."

Sandy and Joe Lee didn't talk anymore about Matt being gay. The radio was on, and they both were singing. It was their favorite song, "Key Largo" by Bertie Higgins.

"I wonder whatever happened to him. He wrote most of his music. I have both of his albums. 'Candle Dancer' is my second favorite."

She dropped Joe Lee off and went back to the motel. It was the first time in a long time that she didn't want a drink. She had eaten so much that she felt like a beached whale. Lying on the bed, she was humming 'Candle Dancer' and drifted off to sleep. When she woke, it was morning. She went to work feeling refreshed. She only had one drink before leaving the motel. Arriving at work, the parking lot was only half full. Mary met her at the counter.

"I don't think we're going to be too busy. It looks like everyone is still full of turkey and staying home. If you want, you can have the day off."

Sandy had been making good tips so she could afford not to work one day. "Yes, I would love that."

She really didn't want to spend the day at the motel. She knew she would just end up drinking all day. She did go to the motel for one little drink and then drove to the dog shelter. She had forgotten that starting today began the promotion to adopt a pet. She went inside and found Mr. Hargraves.

"I have today off, and I thought you might need a little extra help with so many people here to adopt."

"That's very kind of you. Yes, I could use the help, especially with all the paperwork." He took her over to a table and showed her the forms that needed to be filled out for each pet adoption. It wasn't long before people had picked out their pet and the paperwork needed to be finished before they could leave. It was noisy. With all the children and barking dogs, she found it hard to hear. She handed the forms out and let the people fill them out. Then she did the part finalizing the adoption. This method seemed to work quite well. The line moved quickly. The day was over before she knew it. She wondered if Matt was there. She didn't know that he had been working in the back all day, helping people look for just the right pet. As she headed for the bathroom, Matt rounded the corner.

"I thought you had to work today."

"It was so slow Mary gave me the day off. I didn't want to spend it alone, and this is the only other place that I feel comfortable. Would you like to go and get a bite to eat?"

"Yes, I haven't eaten all day."

"Me neither."

They went to a little Italian bistro. Sandy asked him if it was OK if she had a glass of wine. "Sure, I can't wait until the day that we can go out together and toast to our future." Sandy was taken back by what he said. She knew that they had an attraction for one another, but she never thought about a future. With all the things that had happened in her life, she took each day as it came. The best of plans never seem to work out. It didn't make much sense to her to look too far into the future.

"The cook's girlfriend that you were talking to at the dinner."

"Don't pussyfoot around with me. I could tell that you knew her daughter was my child."

Sandy said it was apparent she had the same green eyes.

"Green eyes are not that common. Alexei and I lived together. When I went to prison, she didn't know she was pregnant. She met Norman and he fell in love with her. He didn't care that she was pregnant with someone else's child. Norman loves the both of them and has made them a home. She feels safe and secure. That is the most important thing when you have a child. I can't offer her anything. I have to let my past go for the sake of all of us. I am truly thankful that she and my daughter are okay. She told me that they were going to get married and Norman· was going to adopt Lana. I had a terrible childhood with parents that fought all the time. They never really paid any attention to me. I want my child to grow up in a better environment than I did."

They finished eating and Sandy drove him back to the shelter. Matt went to kiss her goodbye and she pulled away. "I love that we care about each other, but for now, the future is so far away. I would rather just take one day at a time and see where it leads us. Having expectations puts too much pressure on what we have." Then she leaned in and gave him a kiss. As he got out of the car, she said, "I care a lot about you". She was afraid of letting herself get too close emotionally to anyone after that disaster with Wayne.

Her thoughts drifted back to Wayne. He seemed so sincere. She just couldn't imagine what happened to make him change his mind. She wished she hadn't torn his card up. She tried not to let herself dwell on the matter. No matter what she thought, it was probably not true. The only one that knew the truth was Wayne. His words rang so sweet that she couldn't help but believe him. After the facts, it made it hard to believe anything that had to do with love and a man's word. That might not be fair to Matt or not even to herself. Life has a way of shaping your thoughts. She hoped with all her heart that one day she would be able to trust a man. Only the future would reveal if that would be possible.

All of a sudden, she thought about her old life. She wondered what Dr. Can Crusher was doing and if he had missed her. She would have to give him a call to let him know that she was still in the area. Circumstances had prevented her from calling him earlier or coming by. It wouldn't be long before she would be free to do what she wanted. It was at that moment that she realized she would go back to her old life. She missed not being able to do drugs. Not to have the adventure of the experimenting with all types of sex. These thoughts made her feel so horny, something she hadn't felt in a long time. That night at the motel, she fantasized and masturbated and had an orgasm that was so wonderful she wondered how she had gone so long without one.

She hoped the Saturday morning breakfast club of older men would be coming in. They loved to joke with her. She found that they loved her sense of humor and that she joked right back. They always left her a really good tip. Taking yesterday off, she was hoping that the restaurant would be busy. The busier, the better, the more money. The parking lot was full. Apparently, people had gotten over there turkey comas. She hurried in and went straight to her station. The breakfast club had just come in. She greeted them and took them to a table where she could wait on them.

"I hope that all of you had a good Thanksgiving."

One by one, they said it was wonderful to be with family, but they were glad when everyone left. Richard, one of the guys, said, "I have eight grandchildren and they were all there. I love them, but once a year having them all together is planning. A couple of the other men agreed with him. Another one of them, Peter, said I'm a grumpy old son of a bitch. I don't like kids. They're a pain in the ass?"

Sandy asked him, "How many grandchildren do you have?"

"None. I never got married, and I didn't have any kids and I like it that way. No one bossing me around. Several of the other guys said they wish they had made that decision."

Sandy took their order, and as she left, she said to Peter, "Now don't go running off and getting married." All the old guys found that to be quite funny and had a good laugh, even Peter.

The day went by quickly. She made enough tips to make up for the day she had taken off. Each week, she had put aside a little money. On New Year's Eve, she would be done with her probation. She wanted to start the new year with a new place to live. She wondered if her friendship with Matt and Joe Lee would go by the wayside like all her other friends. She didn't know what she would do for New Year's Eve, but being free and able to do anything she wanted, she was sure that it would be something spectacular. She couldn't imagine doing anything that great with Matt and Joe Lee. They still had obligations to the court.

16

Her probation would be up on December 28. She would spend Christmas with Matt and Joe Lee. It would be her farewell to them even though they didn't know it. Going back to her old life, they would not be able to join her. They both were still on probation. She loved them like she had loved so many other people in her life, but all good things come to an end.

She wanted to call Dr. Crusher to see what he was doing on New Year's Eve. Now that she was thinking about being free, she couldn't wait to do a couple of lines of cocaine. She wanted to see if he could arrange for Red and him to get together with her to have one big blowout on New Year's Eve. Just thinking about it made her all wet. She had forgotten how much she had missed sex. Sex and drugs are what she wanted to do while bringing in the new year.

She gave Robert's office a call. "Alias Dr. Can Crusher," his receptionist answered.

"Is it possible that I can speak to the doctor? This is an emergency."

"Hold on. I'll see if he's free."

In a minute or so, he came to the phone. She sang out, "Doctor, Doctor, I think I'm going to crash. Can you help me?"

He answered, "Where the hell have you been? I haven't been able to get you off my mind since the last time we saw each other."

"My life has been a little complicated lately. I was calling to see if you were free New Year's Eve. I thought that maybe you could get a hold of Red, and we could all bring the new year in with a bang."

"That's the best thing I've heard in a long time. I've missed you."

"So it's a date."

"Yes. Can I see you before that?"

"No, I'm afraid I'm a little tied up. I promise you New Year's Eve will be one you won't ever forget."

"I'll arrange for Red to meet us at my house around ten o'clock."

"That's perfect."

"Believe me I can't wait."

"Just make sure you have a lot of that white powder."

"Don't worry. I'll have more than the three of us could possibly do."

"How about a little laughing gas for old time's sake?"

"I think I can arrange that."

"Miss you, see you New Year's Eve."

It was December 8. Her last visit with her probation officer would be December 23 because the offices would be close during the holidays. The six months had gone by so quickly that it didn't even seem much of a punishment. She had enjoyed her time at the shelter—meaning, Joe Lee and Matt had been a God-sent. Working at the shelter with both of them had made her time on probation seem like nothing. It would be hard to leave the both of them behind. She knew that would be the best thing for both of them. She did her time. Now it was time for her to live her life as she wanted.

She loved her job at the restaurant. She thought she would've missed her life at the beauty shop, but she realized that not one of her customers were really her friends. They were just a means to a paycheck. Not one of them called to find out if she was okay and what had really happened.

She imagined that they would step over your dead body to get their hair finished. None of the girls at the shop bothered to call her not, even Terry. That made her a nonbeliever of friends forever.

She was making enough money to save a little each month. She was hoping to move to a better place after the new year. She was so good at sex that she even thought about being a prostitute but much higher class with a price tag that would match. Dr. Crusher had missed her. Maybe he would be able to contribute to her new lifestyle. He might even know a few more men that would like to have sex with someone with her talent and the willingness to experiment with all kinds of sex as long as it didn't cause any bodily harm.

The days flew by, and the restaurant was extremely busy with all the snowbirds. It was the day before Christmas, and after work, they had a little celebration for just the employees. James and Lucy handed out Christmas bonuses. They each got fifty dollars. Sandy was surprised. She had never had a boss give to her at Christmas. The restaurant would be closed on Christmas. It was one of the few days that they were closed. She and Matt and Joe Lee had made plans to meet at Joe Lee's apartment. She was anxious to meet Joe Lee's roommate. She had heard so many good things about him. They were going to rent scary sci-fi movies and order in pizza and Chinese. Sandy had taken some of her savings and had bought Joe Lee and Matt and even a little something for Joe Lee's roommate Martin. She bought Joe Lee a pair of thigh-high boots that a lady had worn into the shelter and she had admired. She bought Matt a watch. It was symbolic for the time that they had spent together and for all the time that she wished for him to have a happy life. Joe Lee had mentioned that Martin was a Frank Sinatra fan, so she bought him *The Manchurian Candidate*, one of Frank's best movies. Joe Lee was really struggling with making enough money to pay her share of the apartment. She gave Sandy a box of chocolate-covered cherries. Sandy was very touched that she had remembered the story; she had told her about her mother buying her a box of them every Christmas. It was her favorite. That box of chocolates meant more to her than any other thing that she could have given her. Matt bought her a silver necklace that said "friends." It was so thoughtful of him that she would cherish it forever. Martin made them each a tin of homemade Christmas cookies.

She was surprised how beautifully the apartment had been decorated. Martin worked at a wholesale furniture store. He was able to get things below cost once a year when they had an employee sale. She had been daydreaming about her new apartment. She really didn't have any talent in decorating. She thought that she might ask Martin to help her when she got her new place.

It was time now to eat and watch sci-fi and be merry. She forgot all about the future and just enjoyed the time she had with her friends. It was one of the best Christmases that she could remember in a long time. Everyone was genuine with their feelings. There was no mass, just friends sharing an evening. She was having second thoughts about leaving their friendship behind. Only time would tell what would happen in the future. She decided not to think about it anymore and just embrace the future and whatever it had in store for her. She had always been the type of person that flew by the seat of the pants. After her father died, her mother was institutionalized, and she had a failed marriage. There wasn't any reason to look too far into the future. As Caesar said, the die has been cast. What will be, will be.

She got back to the motel around two o'clock. She took off her clothes and just left her panties and bra on. She poured herself a tall drink and thought about what a lovely evening she had. She was tempted to dig up one of her little helpers. She only had three more days to go and test-clean one more time. She made herself another drink. After drinking it, she drifted off into a peaceful sleep. She dreamed that she was a child. That Santa had come and had left her everything that she had asked for in the letter that she had sent to him. The smell of the fresh Christmas tree and the color of the lights that adorned it. She could smell the ham and apple pie cooking and sitting on her father's lap. Her father always gave her a special gift just from him to her. A gold locket that had his and her pictures in it and inscribed on the back "The best daughter I could ask for" and the date.

When she had awakened the next morning, sadness washed over her. There was no tree, no smell of ham or pie, and no special gift from her father. The wonderful time she had had the night before seemed to vanish. Loneliness sat in and paralyzed her. She pulled the covers up over her head and decided that she would sleep the day away. She woke up every few hours and had a drink then went right back to sleep. She dreamed of falling and trying to grab things that didn't exist anymore. When morning finally came, she only felt emptiness. That no matter how hard she tried to fill that black hole with happiness, it was always only temporary.

It was time for her to get back to reality, being on her own, not able to rely upon anyone. She had to accept her fate or go crazy. She got up and dressed and went to work. She put a smile on her face even though it was a mask of bravado. She had been placed at the station that was closest to the windows. She saw Wayne's truck drive by and she knew she wasn't dreaming. What was he doing trying to torture her? She wanted to get lost in the world that drugs provided. Not thinking, only living for the moment. Two more days and she would be free at last.

She left work and drove as fast as she could to the motel. She might not be able to do any drugs right now, but she could drink vodka. She had a new bottle. She took it and placed it on the nightstand beside her bed. She took off all her clothes and turn the air conditioning down to sixty-nine. She was hoping in between the cold and the vodka, she would simply go numb. Not able to think of anything. Not to feel the disappointment that she had in her heart. Not feel the loneliness of not having a family. She missed her father more than anyone could ever understand. He had been the perfect man. He had loved her, had cherished her, and had lavished her with gifts. If only somehow she could get that back in her life, but tomorrow would be December 27 only two days to go. She was so busy at work that the two days flew by quickly.

It was finally the twenty-eighth, and the work day was over. It was time to go to Mrs. Fisher's office and be drug tested for the last time. She thought that she would have to go back to court. She called and talked to Mr. Hargraves and found out that as long as the shelter and Mrs. Fisher sent her paperwork in, saying that she had completed her hours and had passed all her drug testing that everything would be over.

When she got to Mrs. Fisher's office, there were quite a few cars in the parking lot. Lots of people were to be drug tested before the holiday. She went and took a seat. It was forty-five minutes before she got to go back and see Mrs. Fisher. She did the usual routine. When Mrs. Fisher completed her test and it was negative, she told Sandy how proud she was of her. She wanted her to keep up the good work and that she hoped she would never see her again. Sandy thanked her and told her that she appreciated her kind words. As she walked out to her car, she felt an overwhelming emotion of relief. She knew as soon as she got back to the motel and the sun set that she would be digging up her little helpers. She could feel the excitement of just the thought of taking a couple of them. Her mouth was dry, and her heart was pounding. Her adrenaline was rushing. She had not felt this kind of excitement for a long time.

She pulled into the motel parking lot and the sun was setting. There were a few people walking around so she would have to wait. It seemed as if there was an unusual amount of people going back and forth to their rooms. Some of them were loading their cars and checking out. She went to her room and poured herself a drink. She was so anxious and full of anticipation that it was hard for her to sit still. She kept going to the window and looked out. She felt like she wanted to open the door and scream for all of them to go away. It wasn't until nine o'clock that the parking lot emptied out. She dug up her little helpers and hurried back into her room. The bottle had been there so long they were covered with dirt. She took them to the sink and wipe them off with a wet paper towel. Opening one of the bottles, dirt fell inside from around the rim. She emptied the entire bottle out on her bed and carefully wiped each one of them off. She took two of them and put the rest back. She put them in a jacket pocket that was hanging in the closet. She felt safer when they were buried in the front garden. She didn't feel like the hassle of having to dig them up. It was hard for her to relax. For six months, she had to be so careful, and now that it was over, she still had that paranoid feeling. She could already start to feel the effects of the pills. She finished drinking her drink and lay down on the bed. The room started to spin. She felt sick to her stomach. Her body had not had that kind of drugs in six months. She wished she had only taken one. It was too late now. She would simply have to stay lying down until the spinning and dizziness went away. With all that anticipation of being able to take them again, it wasn't like she remembered. At that moment, she wondered what was so great about them. The spinning finally stopped. She got up and made her way to the bathroom. Still filling sick, she threw up. She went back to her bed, stumbling. She fell into it. She didn't remember much after that. She fell asleep and didn't wake up until eight thirty. She was in a panic. She was already a half hour late for work. She threw on some clean clothes and hurried off to work.

Mary was waiting at the door. "I was so worried about you. You've never been late before."

"I'm sorry I overslept. I forgot to set my alarm. I hope this didn't cause too much of a problem."

"No, it has happened to all of us at least once. I have given you the station in the front. Just take over when a new party comes in."

She walked to the front of the restaurant and she thought she was still dreaming. Wayne's truck was parked across the street. She couldn't imagine what kind of game he was playing. He knew that she would probably see it. She wanted to run across the street and wait for him to come back. She wouldn't say anything. She would just slap him across the face and then turn and casually walk back to the restaurant. New customers were coming in, and her tables were filling up. She didn't have any more time to waste on thinking what kind of a sick bastard he was. After waiting on a few tables, when she looked back, his truck was gone.

She still felt a little sick to her stomach. The day was busy but it seemed to drag. She couldn't wait to get off. She wanted to eat a warm bowl of soup and then go home and go back to bed. She would wait a while before taking any more of the pills. She guessed the tolerance that her body had built up to them had worn off. The next time she would only take one. The soup of the day was chicken noodle, just what the doctor ordered her. After eating it, she felt much better. Driving home, she couldn't help but wonder what the hell Wayne was doing. When she got home, she didn't even have a drink. She simply took off her clothes and went to bed.

The restaurant would stay open its usual twenty-four hours a day. They had decorated it with balloons and streamers and little tea-arrows for the women and a noise maker for the men. Mary asked her if she would like to work an extra half a shift. That would be four to eight and she declined. She was sure that would be one of the slowest times. Everybody would go home to get ready to go out. But she thanked Mary for thinking about her.

She told herself that she needed to be careful of how much cocaine she did. She didn't want to end up sick and ruining the whole evening. To her surprise, Matt and Joe Lee were waiting for her outside in the parking lot after work.

"Hi, guys. What are you doing here?"

"We haven't heard from you since Christmas eve. We were just wondering what kind of plans we could all make for New Year's Eve."

"Oh, I'm so sorry, but I already have plans."

Matt looked at her. "What do you mean you have plans, without us?"

"Yes, I have a lot of friends that I haven't seen for the last six months.

We are going to get together at a friend's house. My friend is quite a private person. I can't invite you. It is by invitation only from him. I didn't tell them about the trouble I had gotten into. They don't know anything about me being on probation and I want to keep it that way."

Matt had a very disappointed look on his face. Joe Lee just stared down at the ground. She looked up at Sandy with a smile. "How about New Year's Day? I could cook us some black-eyed peas for good luck."

Sandy said, "That sounds wonderful, but I plan on having a huge hangover."

"Then we'll make it in the evening."

"I can't promise that I will show up, but I'll try."

Matt asked her to walk over to his motorcycle. He wanted to talk to her alone. "I thought we had a future together?"

Sandy gave him a hug. "I tried to explain to you that I don't look too far into the future. All my plans that I have ever made have never worked out. So I have decided to let life take me wherever and just try to enjoy the time I have left on this planet."

"Does that mean that we don't have any future?"

"I don't really know. Only time will tell. You still have a year of probation. Joe Lee has two more months. She still won't have a driver's license. Talk about driving, did you both come here on your motorcycle?"

"Yes."

"I have a phobia about motorcycles. I could never ride on one of them."

Matt asked, "Why is that?"

"I had a dear friend that was engaged, and she and her fiancé went to bike week. On the way back, a drunk man hit them. He was killed and she lost one of her legs. Ever since then, it has even been hard for me to look at one."

Matt smiled at her. "If you would just take one little ride with me, I am sure you would change your mind."

"No, I won't ever get on one. I wouldn't even take a ride around the parking lot. That's how frightened I am."

Joe Lee had gotten tired of waiting and walked over to them.

"Well, do we have plans for New Year's day?"

"No, not exactly."

"We have to go. Call one of us and let us know if you're coming."

"I'll do that. Even if I don't come, I will see you sometime in the new year."

She gave each of them a hug and a kiss goodbye. She really didn't know what would happen in the new year. She was hoping for only good things for all of them.

She had already asked for New Year's day off. Maybe she would take it nice and slow on New Year's Eve. She wondered if she had jumped the gun with Dr. Crusher and Red. She had to admit that it was a spur-of-the- moment thought. She realized that the girl that started probation was not the girl she was now. She was a combination of the new and the old. The old her wanted to party, do drugs, and engage in all kinds of sex. The new her was more caring about people in general. She really didn't want to lose Joe Lee's and Matt's friendship. It was different from all her others. Their relationship wasn't based on what she could do for them. All her male relationships had revolved around sex. Matt seemed to really be in love with her. The most that they had done was kiss. Sweet, gentle kisses not the hard, passionate kind that always led up to sex.

She left work and drove to Joe Lee's. She had written her a note, saying how much she appreciated her offering to cook black-eyed peas for all of them.

> Your sweet gesture and kind heart have reminded me
> of what friendship should mean. I promise I'll be at
> your house New Year's day at four. I will bring dessert.
> Please let Matt know that it will be my pleasure to
> spend the first day of the new year with people that
> genuinely care about one another.

She went back to the motel and took a bath. She wanted to take a nap before getting ready to go to Robert's. She drifted off to sleep. When she woke, it was seven thirty. She threw on a blouse and jeans and drove to the barbecue place that was close to the motel. She got fries and a side order of coleslaw and a large Coke. She wasn't in the mood to eat any meat She went back to the motel, and while she ate, she was letting her curling iron heat up. She wanted to do something different with her hair and makeup. She would wear her black lace dress and stilettos and curl and tease her hair and make it look wild and windblown and would do a smoky eye with liner that made her eyes look like a cat and black mascara and ruby red lips and a little deeper shade of blush for her cheeks.

17

She left the motel at nine thirty. She wanted to get there a little early before Red showed up. She wasn't sure why, but she had an uncomfortable feeling about the three of them getting together. The new her was trying to convince her to just drive away. The old her wanted to feel that adrenaline rush that came with sex and drugs. The old her won out. She parked the car a block away from his house like she had done the last time. When she got to his house, the door was cracked open so she went in and left it ajar like she had found it.

"Robert, are you here?"

She thought she heard his voice coming from his bedroom. She went to his room. The drapes and sliding glass doors that led to his pool were open.

"Come on out here. I have a little sample of your favorite white powder to get this party rolling."

She joined him on the patio. He had a line waiting for her. All that logic about taking it easy went straight out of her head. She took his little gold straw and inhaled. In just seconds, she felt that old familiar feeling.

"That stuff is really great, but I need a little vodka. You know where it is in the freezer. Pour one for me and Red. She should be here any minute. You did leave the door open?"

"Yes."

Before she got the third drink poured, she felt a hand on her back, and Red whispered in her ear, "I couldn't wait to see you again."

She turned around and tried to hand Red a drink, but before she took it from her, she leaned in and gave Sandy a wet, passionate kiss. The old Sandy was back in control. She took the drink back and placed it on the counter. She grabbed Red by her hips and pulled her even closer. She kissed her back, and they just stood in the kitchen, making out like two lost lovers. After, they took the drinks to the patio and joined Robert. He took his little brown bottle of white powder and made three lines. Red took the gold straw and snorted hers first then Sandy. Robert made another line.

"I think I'm a little behind you two. It looked like you had already gotten the party started in the kitchen. I better catch up." He snorted both lines. They all raised their glasses and did a toast to old friends getting back together. All of them drank the vodka straight down. Sandy stood up.

"Do you need a refill?"

She gathered the glasses and walked to the kitchen. She could hear Red and Robert talking in the background, something about filming the night's activities. Sandy poured them all another drink and went back to the patio.

"I thought I heard you guys talking about making a movie of tonight. I'm not comfortable with that. If you want me to film the two of you, that will be fine. I really don't want to be on camera."

Robert took a sip out of his drink. "Why not?"

"How do I know what will happen in the future? That film might just end up on the internet."

Robert laughed, "I will have the only copy, and you know I wouldn't do that."

"No, you can't change my mind. If this is a deal breaker for tonight, I guess I'll have to leave."

Red grabbed her hand. "No, no, if you don't want to join in with us, you can film just the two of us."

Sandy looked at them. "No kidding around. I really do mean I don't want any pictures taken of me."

Robert took the bottle out again and made three more lines. After they were done and had drank their vodka, they moved inside to his bedroom. He had handcuffs, a whip, blindfolds, and several adult toys. A movie camera was set up on a tripod a few feet away from the foot of the bed. He handed Sandy the remote for the camera.

"You can start and stop it whenever you want. Will that satisfy you?"

"Yes."

"Then take off your clothes and join me in bed." He was naked by the time the girls got undressed.

After joining him on the bed, he told Red to handcuff him and put a blindfold on him. Red was to start whipping him and Sandy was to film it. Red had him roll over and put his hands behind his back. She put the handcuffs on him tight. Sandy took the remote and started filming. Red started off gently hitting his backside. He told her to do it harder and harder. Red seemed to enjoy whipping him. They both started moaning, and then Red picked up the pace. At that point, he was screaming in between the moans, and then came a high-pitched scream from Red. He rolled over and told Sandy to get on top and ride him as hard as she could. She turned the remote off and climbed on top. She had to admit that she was excited. It didn't take long before the two of them were moaning and screaming in ecstasy. Red uncuffed Robert, and the three of them lay on the bed.

"I don't know about you two girls, but that was fucking fantastic." They were still out of breath but managed to agree with him.

After lying there for a while, the three of them thought it would be refreshing to take a swim.

Sandy said, "Last one in is a rotten egg and doesn't get any more cocaine all night." The three of them were stumbling over each other to get to the pool first. They all managed to jump in at the same time.

"I guess there's no rotten egg, so what do you ladies say when we get out we all do a couple more lines and keep this party going?"

After about a ten-minute swim, Sandy went and refilled their glasses. Robert's little bottle was out of powder. Sandy brought the drinks out to the patio. He told them both to just wait there and he'd be right back. He liked both of the girls, but he knew never to trust a drug addict. He didn't want them to see where he kept his stash. He returned in just a few minutes. The bottle was full again. He laid out three long lines, and they each took a turn snorting them.

"Do either of you girls have a suggestion? Something you'd really like to do?"

Red said, "I'd like Sandy to film us. You can tie me up and blindfold me and spank my bottom till it turns red. Then get up behind me and fuck me as hard as you can."

Red smiled at Sandy. "Are you sure you don't want to join in?"

"I don't have to be on camera to get my jollies off. I'll have fun filming the two of you. I guess I have a little voyeur in me. If I get really turned on, I'll put the camera on automatic and masturbate."

Robert handcuffed and blindfolded Red. Sandy started the camera rolling. She decided to put it on automatic and lay down on the carpeted floor. She spread her legs wide and began to masturbate. She didn't realize how much enjoyment she got out of watching the two of them. She had never done that before. She had always been a willing participant. She had never sat on the sidelines and just watched. It was a grand finale. The screaming that came from the house should have been heard by the neighbors—it was so loud.

After the three of them had drunk almost two bottles of vodka and done more cocaine than they should have and had exhausted themselves with wild sex, the three of them passed out on Robert's bed. He had closed the sliding glass doors and shut the blinds. It was dark in the room. Sandy was the first one to wake up. She glanced at the clock. It was one thirty in the afternoon. She felt like hell. She didn't know which hurt the worst, her head or her pussy. She really couldn't remember all the things that they had done. Apparently, the sex toys were involved. Probably the big oversized black dildo. She decided not to wake Red or Robert. She gathered her clothes, putting them on quickly and left. Walking to her car, she was thinking if she had really had a good time. She was having a hard time walking. It felt like a groin muscle had been pulled. She not only had a horrible, pounding headache, but her mouth was dry and pasty and taste like something had died in it. There was an old bottle of warm water in her car. She used all of it to rinse her mouth. She drove back to the motel. She wanted to take a shower and brush her teeth. She would take some of her pain pills and go back to sleep. She set her alarm clock for five. She was hoping that she would feel well enough to go to Joe Lee's for black-eyed peas.

She dreamed of strange men chasing her. Trying to grab her. She was terrified. Every time she thought she was safe, another crazed man would appear. He would chase her deeper into a wooded area that had many different kinds of plants that seem to reach out and grab her and throw her to the ground. She would get back up not willing to give in. Then more men would appear. Some looked like her husband, some like Mr. X, even Wayne and Dr. Can Crusher Robert. There would be two or three of them coming at her from all directions. They all had a fist full of money. They would chase after her, calling her a whore and a murderer. The faster she run, the more men would appear. She would find a house and bang on doors, asking them to help her, but no one answered her pleas. She had no choice but to keep running. She was naked, and the woods scraped against her skin, making it bleed. She was exhausted. She couldn't run any more. She fell to the ground, blood dripping in her eyes. She had a pill bottle full of painkillers and a bottle of vodka. She sat on the cold ground. It began to rain.

Parts of her life ran through her mind. She remembered when she was a little girl how she loved to play in the rain. Her grandmother would always say if the sun was shining and it was raining, the devil was beating his wife. She felt like the devil was beating her. She dropped the bottle of pills, and they rolled all over the ground. She found as many as she could and took them. She drank the bottle of vodka.

She lay down and whispered to herself, "I won't wake up. The nightmare will be over."

Rose had other plans. She wasn't willing to stand by and let Sandy die. She kept screaming inside her head, "Wake up, wake up!"

Part of what Sandy was experiencing was a dream. Part of it might be a glimpse into the future. Her heart was racing. It was beating over a hundred. Her blood pressure was steadily rising. She was covered with sweat, but she felt cold and clammy. Rose could feel Sandy dying. It was no dream. Suddenly, Sandy opened her eyes. She was gasping for air and was cold as ice. She felt she had been ripped from her grave.

That same strange feeling swept over her that she wasn't alone. Then the same warm breeze filled the room. Her chill vanished. She didn't know how it was possible that someone was with her. Someone or something had saved her life. She thought she must have a guardian angel that would keep her safe if she would just listen to that little voice in her head. Then suddenly her mood changed. She screamed out loud, "Am I going mad like my mother? Can you hear me?" There was only silence and the warm breeze seemed to disappear.

She looked at the clock. It was eight thirty. She took a hot shower. The warm water made her feel much better. She dressed and decided to hurry and go to Joe Lee's. She might be too late for black-eyed peas, but with all that had happened, she didn't want to be alone.

When she reached Joe Lee's apartment, Matt's motorcycle was parked in the driveway. Hurrying to the door, the heel of her shoe caught in a crack. She fell, scraping her elbow and hitting her head. She saw stars and, for a moment, blacked out. Matt thought he saw her car pull up. He was going outside to greet her when he saw her fall. He rushed to her side, lifting her off the sidewalk and carrying her into the house. The blood from the scrapes stained his shirt. Joe Lee ran and got an old towel and put it on the couch.

"Lay her down here."

A big black-and-blue goose egg formed right above her temple. Joe Lee got ice from the freezer and wrapped it in a dish cloth. When she went back to the living room, she gave the ice to Matt. He held it against her head. Martin went to the bathroom and got a wet washcloth and a bandage to fix Sandy's bleeding elbow. Sandy was still not fully conscious. She was mumbling as if she were having a fight with someone. After holding the ice on the goose egg for ten minutes, Sandy slowly opened her eyes. She looked up at Matt.

"Who are you and where am I?"

"Sandy, it's Matt."

Joe Lee leaned over the back of the couch. "Sandy, it's Joe Lee."

Sandy tried to sit up but she was still too shaken and weak. "I don't know why you keep calling me Sandy. My name is Rose." Matt, Joe Lee, and Martin looked at each other. You could tell there were confusion by the looks on their faces.

Matt told Sandy, "I assure you your name is not Rose."

Sandy managed to wiggle up in a sitting position. "I don't know who you people are and I don't know why I am here, but the one thing I am sure of is my name is Rose. I still don't understand. Who are you people and why am I here?"

"We are your friends. We had made plans for you to meet us here around five o'clock for black-eyed peas. You didn't show up until just a few minutes ago. You were walking up the sidewalk and fell and hit your head. We brought you in the house and bandage your bleeding elbow and put ice on the big lump on your head where you hit it."

"I don't remember. Thank you for being so kind to me, but I'm telling you the truth. I don't know who you are and my name is Rose."

The three of them left Sandy on the couch and went into the kitchen.

"What are we going to do now?" Joe Lee asked.

Matt looked at Joe Lee. "I don't know."

Martin thought it would be best to either call an ambulance or take her to the hospital. "We don't want to be responsible if she has bleeding on the brain and we didn't do anything." There was a consensus that they should take her to the hospital. They went back to the living room and Sandy was gone.

They ran outside. Her car was still there. Matt told Joe Lee and Martin that they needed to find her. "She's out there, stumbling around in the dark, not even knowing who she really is."

They spread going in different directions, searching for her. Martin found her five blocks away, walking in the middle of the street. He approached her with caution. He didn't want to scare her and make her run.

When he reached her, he said in a very calm voice, "Rose, I think you may be really hurt. Let me take you to the hospital so they can do a CAT scan and make sure that everything is okay."

Reluctantly, she let him take her hand and guide her back to the house. Matt and Joe Lee were waiting there. "You found her."

"She was walking in the middle of the street." He gave them both a wink. "I told Rose that she should let us take her to the hospital to make sure that there is no internal bleeding." Matt went through Sandy's purse and found the car keys. They took her purse and put her in the back seat of the car. Joe Lee got in on the other side. Martin drove and Matt rode shotgun. The hospital was about twenty minutes away. The longer they were in the car, the more agitated Sandy got. At one point, she was screaming for them to stop and let her out, that they were kidnapping her. Joe Lee tried to calm her and assure her that they only wanted to help her.

"The right thing to do was to go to the hospital and make sure that you're okay."

When they reached the hospital, Joe Lee helped Sandy out of the back seat. Matt went into the hospital to get a wheelchair. When he returned, Sandy was very irritated and refused to sit in it.

"I don't know why you brought me here. I don't need a hospital." The three of them begged her to go inside and let a doctor make sure that everything was okay. Matt touched Sandy on the lump on her head.

She immediately said, "Stop that hurts."

"That's my point. You hit your head. You can't remember and you have a knot on your head the size of a goose egg. Please let us take you inside."

Sandy reluctantly sat down in the wheelchair and let Matt take her into the hospital waiting room. He took her purse to the nurse's station and explained that she had hit her head and she seemed to have some form of amnesia.

"Her name is Sandy Nash. It says so right here on her driver's license. She insists that her name is Rose and she has no idea who we are. We have all known each other for almost a year. We met doing volunteer work at the dog shelter."

The nurse asked if they knew if she had any relatives—mother or father or sister or brother that lived in the area. Matt told the nurse that she was an only child, her father was dead, and her mother was in a mental facility about fifty miles away called Chattahoochee. The nurses told him that she was familiar with that institution.

The nurse called for help to take Sandy back to one of the examining rooms. By the time they got to her, she was furious, calling all of them kidnappers.

"They brought me here against my will. I don't even know these people. They keep calling me Sandy, but my name is Rose."

The nurse assured her that she was in good hands, and they were going to find out what had happened and all the circumstances that led up to her accident.

Sandy started screaming, "Help me! help me! I'm being held against my will."

Two male nurses came out, and as gently as they could, they restrained her. Once they got to one of the cubicles in the emergency room, another nurse came in with a shot. The male nurse held Sandy's arm still while the other nurse administered the shot.

"This is going to help you relax and make the pain go away."

They took her from the wheelchair and put her into a bed. Then they put restraining straps on her wrist to make sure that she didn't try to get out of bed or hurt herself. They took the bed to an elevator that led to the area where they could take a CAT scan.

18

The shot relaxed Sandy, and she drifted off to sleep. The nurse would only let one go back with her. They decided that Joe Lee would be less intimidating being a woman. It was twenty minutes before Dr. Bloom came to examine her.

He said, "We will know more once we get the CAT scan back. Until then, I think it's best that we keep her sedated. The nurse will give you an identification number for the patient. You must use this number when you call to find out any information. You might as well go home and just give the nurses station a call in the morning. The nurse told me that the only living relative she has is her mother who has been institutionalized in a mental facility. Do you know how long she has been there?"

Joe Lee looked at Dr. Bloom. "I've only known her for a year. She rarely ever talked about her mother. I think she has been there for quite some time."

Joe Lee turned and walked out the door and down the long hallway. Matt and Martin were waiting for her in the waiting room. The doctor said, "We might as well go home. They won't know anything until they can read the CAT scan. He gave me a number that I have to use when I call to find out what is going on." They left the hospital and drove back to the apartment.

The next morning, Joe Lee called the hospital. She read off the identification number that the nurse had given her. They put her through to the nurse's station.

"This is Nurse Collins. How may help you?"

"I'm calling about Sandy Nash—you know the girl that thinks her name is Rose? She came in last night."

"Do you have the ID number for the patient?"

"Yes!"

After telling the nurse the PIN, she got Sandy's chart. "She seems to be quite agitated this morning and has no idea why she is here. She does insist that her name is Rose, but clearly her identification says Sandy Nash. The CAT scan was clear that she had a concussion. This is why she has amnesia. She had a bit of bleeding on the brain in the area that controls memory. This is probably temporary, but there is no guarantee that she will get her past memories back. I have seen in some patients a full recovery within weeks, and on the other hand, I've seen patients that never recover their memory. When the doctor comes in, I will have him give you a call so he can set up an appointment to decide what to do with Sandy Rose—that's what we call her now."

As Joe Lee hung up the phone, the guys were anxiously awaiting any kind of news about Sandy.

"She is still agitated and insist her name is Rose. She doesn't remember falling and she still doesn't remember who we are. The nurse said she may or may not get her full memory back. Only time will tell. Now the doctor must decide what would be best for her. They can't keep her in the hospital waiting for her memory to come back. The doctor is going to call me later. Until then, we just need to go on with our daily activities. Sitting around wondering what might happen won't do any of us any good."

Matt and Martin agreed. "I'm starving. Why don't we all go have breakfast? I know a place that has Sunday brunch." They piled in the car and drove to the restaurant in silence. Once seated inside, the boys ate like there was no tomorrow. Plate after plate of eggs, ham, bacon and waffles, fresh strawberries to top the waffles with. Coffee, tea, hot chocolate, milk sodas, and you could even make your own milkshake. Joe Lee watched them eat. Her appetite was slight. She couldn't get Sandy off her mind and what may happen to her. By the time they got back to the house, there was a message from the doctor.

Joe Lee quickly called the doctor back. Her hands were sweaty with anticipation. Dr. Bloom, to her surprise, answered the phone himself.

"I'm calling about Sandy Nash. You left me a message."

"Yes, I'm sorry to say that there hasn't been any improvement. There isn't anything physically wrong with her. We can't keep her in the hospital. We can't release her without a guardian or relative. I don't believe you would be capable of caring for Sandy in her current condition. We think it's best that she go to a facility where she has twenty-four-hour supervision. I was thinking that it might be helpful to put her in the same institution that her mother is in. Maybe interacting with her mother, a somewhat-familiar face, might help her to get her memory back. Do you know the facility her mother is in?"

"Yes, Chattahoochee, but isn't that for mentally challenged people that will in most cases never return to the life they had before?"

"Yes, in most cases that is true. Sandy has no physical trauma. She doesn't need rehab to learn to walk or talk again. We will be transferring her to the new facility as soon as I can arrange it. I will put you down on the visitors list."

"Matt and Martin are friends of hers also. Can they be put on the visitors list?"

"Yes, I think it would be better for her not to have visitors for at least a week. It takes time for people to get acclimated to their new surroundings. She not remembering you or your friends may make the situation worse. When you do go to see her, try not to say or do anything to upset her. If she thinks her name is Rose, call her Rose. She will have a psychological evaluation when she arrives. That way we can set up a program that will best suit her needs. She will be in the same dorm as her mother. I have to go. I have other patients."

The guys had already left for work, and she had to hurry or she'd be late. News of Sandy would have to wait until the evening. Matt and she were still completing their hours at the dog shelter. Mr. Rosenblum had been very fond of Sandy. Joe Lee thought that she would buy a get-well card and have everyone sign it, not knowing when Sandy would be at her new residence and that they couldn't go right away. Even though she didn't remember them, she still wanted her to know that they cared.

Joe Lee couldn't get Sandy out of her mind, and being preoccupied, the days seem to fly. She stopped and bought a funny get-well card. She didn't want to send anything too serious. It had a dog on the front, and inside, it was a pop-up card and it played a little tune, barking, "You get well, wagging my tail. We all just wanted to tell you get well," it played over and over. When the boys saw it, they couldn't help but just laugh and laugh. Maybe the card would help her remember working at the shelter.

Dr. Bloom had contacted the Chattahoochee facility. He had explained the situation to the admitting provider. There was an opening for a new patent, and it would also be possible to put her in the same housing that her mother was in. The arrangements were made and Sandy would be transferred the next day.

They had sent in a psychologist and social worker to evaluate Sandy and to make her a ward of the court. That meant that they had taken away any of her rights. At that point, she would have no say in her treatment until she could leave and live on her own again. This would all be up to the administrators of Chattahoochee to determine when she would no longer be a threat to herself and have the ability to work and care for herself.

At the hospital the next morning, Dr. Bloom tried to explain to Sandy, or shall we say Sandy Rose, that she was being moved to a new hospital that could better care for her. This sent her into a rage.

"There is nothing wrong with me. I don't know what those strange people told you about me but it's not true. They don't even know me.

Apparently, they know someone that must look similar to me named Sandy. They are confused. Like I said, they don't even know me."

The doctor looked at her and said, "Rose, where do you live and what kind of work do you do?"

There was a long hesitation and then she said, "I'm a hairstylist."

Dr. Broom asked her, "And what is the name of the shop you work for?"

"I can't think of it right now."

"Then where do you live?"

"I'm not sure."

Dr. Benson took Sandy's hand. "You see, Rose, we can't just release you to wander around on the street not knowing where you work or where you live. There are plenty of people out there that would take advantage of someone so fragile as you are now. Where you are going, there will be people there to help you get your memory back."

She looked at him with daggers in her eyes. "Where exactly do you think my memory went?"

"That's what we hope to find out."

She was quite loud. The nurse came in and gave her a shot to calm her down and help her relax and fall asleep. Dr. Bloom wrote in her chart to keep her lightly tranquilized for her own safety. He thought it would be best for everyone for her not to be so anxious during the move to the new facility.

Dr. Bloom had the nurse call Joe Lee to find out if she could go by where Sandy had been staying and let them know that she would no longer be there.

"We would really appreciate it if you could gather her things and if possible keep them for her. Once she is in the new facility, she will need her clothes. Could you take them to her in a few days? She is being transferred tomorrow. For the first three days, she will be evaluated. That will be in the hospital part of the facility. She can wear the hospital gown they provide. Once she is put into the housing, she will need her own clothes."

"I'll be more than happy to."

Dr. Bloom said, "You shouldn't go to see Sandy for at least a week after she's been relocated. You can just leave them with the front check-in, and I will let them know to be expecting you. When you come, you will be able to find out more about the time. About the time when Sandy will be in the general population of her dorm."

Joe Lee drove to the motel after work the next day. The door was locked. She went to the front desk to inform them of Sandy's situation and gather her things. The manager of the motel said, "Normally, we would have to have the permission of Sandy to let you in."

Joe Lee gave the manager the number of Dr. Bloom. "He can explain the situation to you better than I can. I need to gather all of her belongings."

The manager took the number and dialed it. He got the receptionist and asked to speak to Dr. Bloom.

"In reference to what?"

"A patient of hers, Sandy Nash. I have a friend of hers that has come to pick up her clothes and other things. I just need verification that she has been asked by the doctor to retrieve Sandy's belongings."

"I am quite familiar with the case, and yes, Dr. Bloom has asked Joe Lee to go by and let you know that Sandy would no longer be there and take her things."

19

Joe Lee didn't know that she would never see Sandy again. She dropped her things off at the front desk and was told that they would notify her when she was allowed to have visitors. That call never came. The doctors thought it was best that she had no outside contact to her old life. She didn't remember any of it, and she insisted that her name was Rose, not Sandy. They called her Rose, and it seemed to make her less anxious. The evaluation showed that she was paranoid schizophrenic, the same as her mother.

The day came that they were going to put her into the general population. It was quite nice, two people to a bedroom and a large room that everyone could congregate in. The therapist decided to put Sandy in with her mother, Vivian. They were hoping that she did have some recollection of her mother. The first night that she was to stay at the new facility, they gave her mild tranquilizer to keep her from being anxious. The next morning, when they came to the bedroom, Sandy's mother was sitting by her bed, stroking her hair, calling her Rose. This astounded the staff. They had not mentioned that Sandy was her daughter. They couldn't imagine how Vivian knew that Sandy only responded to the name Rose. They were watching from the doorway when Sandy opened her eyes.

"Mother, I have been waiting so long to meet you. Do you know who I am?"

"Yes, my darling, you are my child, Rose." She held and rocked her as if she was a baby. Rose put her thumb in her mouth and started to suck it and make cooing, gurgling noise as if she was an infant.

The staff quickly alerted the psychiatric department to come quickly to observe what they had seen. Dr. Cutter was the head of the department. He hurried to the bedroom door camera in hand. He wanted to document this. He had never seen this phenomenon before and wanted to make a permanent record of it Dr. Cutter chased everyone away. He stood there quietly recording.

Vivian held her for quite a long period of time, rocking her and singing. For the first time, Sandy Rose seemed quite content and fell asleep. Vivian laid her back on the bed and kissed her cheek.

"You are my beautiful Rose, and I have kept you in my heart and in my memory for all these years, knowing that someday we would meet." Vivian looked up and saw Dr. cutter. "What are you doing, spying on us? Don't try to keep us apart. A mother and her child have a right to their privacy. Do not bother us. Can't you see my child is sleeping?"

Dr. Cutter acknowledged Vivian's wishes and stopped filming and walked away from the door. Vivian laid down beside Rose, holding her hand. She fell asleep.

The staff woke them for lunch. Vivian took Rose by the hand and led her to the table. She tucked her napkin under her chin as if it were a bib. She spooned the food into Rose's mouth so very gently you would have thought she was feeding an infant On occasion, she would make a funny face and tell Rose to open the hangar so the plane could go in. With a spoon full of mashed potatoes, Rose opened her mouth and took the food like a hungry baby bird would take it from its mother. Then they both would laugh and then Vivian would repeat saying "open the hangar" over and over again until the plate was empty. She never ate a bite only being concerned that her child was full and happy. The staff didn't interfere. Vivian took Rose by the hand, and they walked to a rocking chair that was in the main room. Vivian sat down and Rose climbed into her lap.

"You want your mommy to rock you? Mommy loves you, and I will never leave you again, I promise." Rose clapped her hands with delight like a small child would and put her arms around her mother and kissed her.

After showing his colleagues what he had recorded, they were all astonished. Dr. Seifert, one of his colleagues was amazed. He had never experienced or witnessed anything like that.

"I think we must approach this case with great care. This could be an opportunity to be published. Groundbreaking research. Everything must be carefully documented. I would love to help you on this exciting project." Dr. Cutter paused for a moment.

"I don't want to make a decision on this at the moment. I think it is best that I just patiently and quietly document their day-to-day activity with one another."

Dr. Seifert said, "Remember I am more than willing and am quite excited about the opportunity to help make such a discovery about the human brain. One of the most fascinating parts of the situation is how the mother recognizes each child as if they were independent of one another."

As Dr. Cutter patiently observed and recorded the interactions between Rose and her mother, he noticed a slight change. It seemed as though Sandy was trying to find her way back. But at this point, Rose was dominant. As the months went by, he could tell Sandy was becoming more of an active part.

One evening when he went to check on Sandy Rose and their mother, Rose and Sandy were interacting with each other. Vivian, their mother, seemed to know the both of them. She would be talking to Rose and then she would recognize that Sandy was talking with her. It was hard for Dr. Cutter to do the rest of his duties. He hated to break away from the interaction between the three of them.

Sandy Roses twenty-eighth birthday was two weeks away. The staff had planned a small party for them. Dr. Cutter wondered who would show up. Would it be Sandy or would it be Rose? With great anticipation, he would have to wait.

Vivian still treated Rose as a small child. She treated Sandy more as an adult. Sandy dressed herself, bathe herself, and had some interaction with the staff and other patients.

Rose would cling to her mother still very childlike. Her mother would help her dress, help her take a bath, and still insisted upon feeding her as if she were an infant.

The two weeks flew by and the staff prepared for the party. They even had two small cakes made. One said, "Happy birthday, Rose," and the other, "Happy birthday, Sandy."

The residents, the staff, and even some of the personnel were invited. Dr. Cutter was quite anxious to see how each one of them would react to the situation. The evening had finally come. Rose was tired after an hour of all the hustle and bustle and wanted to go to bed. Her mother Vivian took her to her room and tucked her in. She was quite tired herself so she went to bed and fell fast asleep.

Around ten o'clock, Sandy rose from her bed dressed and quietly slipped out of the room. Vivian awakened the next morning to find her children's bed was empty.

This is where the characters in the book are today:

John, Sandy's ex-husband, remarried and has three children. He owns his own car repair shop.

Jean, the prostitute, is still working the streets and has been arrested once again for solicitation.

The attorney Mr. Hargraves is still a public defender. Jean continues to be one of his clients.

The restaurant manager Mr. Brady is still on the job.

Mary, the floor manager, had a heart attack and died.

Wayne did fall in love with Sandy at first sight. The day he was to meet her in the parking lot. His son got into a motorcycle accident. Now he couldn't leave his family. His obligations were too great. He did drive by the restaurant on occasions, trying to catch a glimpse of her.

Roman and Kevin are still together. They got legally married. They are in the process of adopting a little girl.

Norman and Sarah got married, and Norman adopted Lana Marie. Sarah is pregnant and due any day.

James and Lucy still own the restaurant and are loved by their employees.

Officer Brown got a promotion and is now a detective working homicides.

Officer Jones was shot and killed by an irate husband when he was on a call for a domestic disturbance.

Loretta Fisher is still a probation office. She is going to AA meetings trying to beat her own addiction.

Mr. Rosenblum still runs the dog shelter.

Robert, alias Dr. Can Crusher, was found naked in his garage dead. His antique Volkswagen had run over him and pinned him to the garage floor. He didn't die from his injuries. He died from dehydration. He was on a week vacation. When he didn't show up for work, one of his assistants went to his home and found the door unlocked. She called the police and that was when he was discovered. The investigation into his death is ongoing.

Red was the one behind the wheel of the Volkswagen. They had gotten together for some kinky sex. She was drunk and high on cocaine when she made the deadly mistake. She panicked. She wiped her fingerprints and moved to Colorado within two days. There was nothing to connect her to him. He had kept his private life totally secret from everyone.

Martin and Joe Lee are still roommates. Joe Lee met a girl named Bonnie at the dog shelter, and they are currently dating. Martin isn't dating anyone particular. He is still working at the furniture store and is their top salesman.

Matt still thinks of Sandy often. He could never find out what really happened to her. He was never allowed to visit her. He is off probation and is currently going to Cordon Blue Culinary Institution. He got a full scholarship from an organization that helps people get back on track after being incarcerated.

Dr. Bloom documented the day-to-day interaction between Vivian and Sandy Rose and hopes to publish his documentary in the near future.

Vivian is still at the institution. She is currently not speaking and is on a hunger strike. The institution is considering putting her on a feeding tube.

They found Don's truck. They never found Don. He is still being considered a missing person.

Sandy Rose, with the help of one of the maintenance men at the institution, managed to escape on her twenty-eighth birthday. She had sex with him in exchange for a bottle of vodka and some pain pills. She ran into the woods that surrounded the institution. Late that night, there was a terrible thunderstorm. When they found her, she was lying in mud and was covered with bug bites. The empty bottle of pills was clutched in her hand and the vodka bottle lay empty beside her: Amazingly, she wasn't dead. She developed pneumonia and died ten days later.

About the Author

Theresa Seifert was born in Dunedin, Florida, and had a career as a hairstylist for thirty-four years. She ran her own business for the last twenty-five years of her career. She was married to John Seifert for twenty- five years. He developed leukemia at the age of thirty-four and died on December 3, 1995, leaving her a widow.

She struggled through her years of school. It took fourteen years to finally graduate high school. When she was in the second grade, they told her mother that she would not be able to learn properly and should be put in special education. Her mother would not allow that to happen. She told them that she may struggle, but she will make it. Thank God for her mother.

Now retired at the age of seventy-one, she is finally able to complete a lifelong dream of being a published author. This was made possible by Dragon software. Unable to spell, it would have been impossible without it. Her advice to anyone that struggles with a disability: don't give up because dreams can come true.